The Madams

The Madams

A Wildly Provocative Novel by
Zukiswa Wanner

Oshun

Oshun

Published by Oshun Books
an imprint of Struik Publishers
(a division of New Holland Publishing (South Africa) (Pty) Ltd)
PO Box 1144, Cape Town, 8000
New Holland Publishing is a member of Johnnic
Communications Ltd.

First published in 2006

1 2 3 5 7 9 10 8 6 4 2

PUBLISHING MANAGER: Michelle Matthews
MANAGING EDITOR: Ceridwen Morris
EDITOR: Jacqui L'Ange
COVER DESIGN: Bridgitte Chemaly
COVER PHOTOGRAPH: George Mahashe
TEXT DESIGN AND TYPESETTING: Bridgitte Chemaly
PRODUCTION MANAGER: Valerie Kömmer

Set in 10 pt on 14 pt ITC Stone Serif

Reproduction by Hirt & Carter (Cape) (Pty) Ltd
Printed and bound by Paarl Print,
Oosterland Street, Paarl, South Africa

ISBN-13: 978 1 77007 058 5
ISBN-10: 1 77007 058 3

About the author

Zukiswa Wanner was born in Lusaka, Zambia to an exiled South African father and a Zimbabwean mother. She went to school in Zimbabwe and studied journalism at Hawai'i Pacific University in Hawai'i.

She now lives and works in the cultural capital of the world, Johannesburg. This is her first novel.

Dedication

To Vusi Vokwana, sister, friend and comrade in the struggle for life. And for my literary fathers: Doc Bikitsha, Lewis Nkosi and ZB Molefe – thanks for pushing.

Contents

Prologue

I love my life.

I love my cute, smart-ass five-year-old son, Hintsa.

I love his witty, beer-gut-lugging father and my significant other, Mandla.

I love my supportive, though sometimes misguided, girlfriends, Nosizwe and Lauren.

I love my job with its business travel perks and the day-to-day challenge it offers on 'how to look busy'. But, there are times ... There are times like now when I get, to paraphrase *The Unofficial Woman's Handbook*, sick and tired of being sick and tired.

I am tired of having to be a Superslave at the office, a Supermom to my son and a Superslut to my man. I am tired of the fact that if I so much as indicate that I need 'Me' time, I have somehow fallen short of the high standards set for me as a modern woman.

I am admitting defeat to my hectic schedule. I am giving in to something I thought I would never do. I'm going to hire a maid.

There, Mother, I've said it. My late mother must be laughing in her grave. I told her that she was pretentious for having a maid when I was growing up. I always maintained that having a maid is really about playing 'madam'. A woman should be able to take care of herself and her own without bringing a stranger into the family. But I have failed to do that without stressing myself out.

Makhulu keeps telling me how happy we sistahs should be that we are living in the age of the liberated woman where we can do what we want. But are we really liberated?

At least in her day the gender roles were clearly defined. Man went to work and brought back money for rent, fees and clothing and woman tended house and her thirty-metre square vegetable patch. Sure, unlike me, that woman did not have a choice about whether to be a professional woman or a housewife, but that choice enslaves my genera-tion because we are still expected to play the traditional roles to perfection. I do not know why my *makhulu* said this to me in any event, because neither she nor my maternal grandmother fits into the 'traditional' box.

It is a sad reality that in South Africa my 'womanity' is still defined by how well I cook and clean and there is still a high-held belief that, should I choose to leave my job, I could do 'other things' (never mind that I am paying half the mortgage!). I am fortunate in that Mandla is a 'renais-sance man' who shares the housework and helps care for Hintsa. Unfortunately, this is only true when none of his rela-tives or his macho, mooching friends from *ekasi* are visiting. When they are around, I have to play my 'womanly role' of cooking, cleaning and going to buy beer for 'the boyz'. I have to clean up any beer they've spilt and disappear to read Hintsa a bedtime story. I hate that Mandla and I have to do this role playing for an audience we do not even like, but as he says, 'You don't want them to say you gave me *korobela* do you?' Frankly, when my hands feel as if they are not part of my body from chopping vegetables, cooking and washing dishes, I really couldn't care less, but I understand his point ... because I know our people.

So I don my Superwoman cape. And what a heavy cape it can be when a laid-back weekend is unceremoniously interrupted by these teflon-coated scavengers who, should we ever – God forbid – hit a rough spot, will give no practical assistance whatsoever. I do not want to get so stressed at trying to play all my roles perfectly that I end up being the one that is used as an example among my peers: 'Girl chill, you don't want to end up like Thandi.' Hence the maid.

Not only does getting a maid make me feel very *bourgeois*, but it also makes me feel like I am exploiting another individual. I have no problem telling my PA she has taken minutes as if she dropped out in Grade Four, but the thought of asking somebody to 'trust pink to get the stains out' on my whites, or have another woman touching my bras ... it gnaws at my social conscience.

One of My Girls, Lauren, has tried to convince me that I have a screwed up mentality for thinking that way. 'Ours is a capitalist nation, my darling,' she intones, 'and you'll just have to live with the pecking order. In any case you will see how good it is to have a maid the moment you employ one. My MaRosie knows the children better than me. In fact, the first word my babies said was, "Rosie".'

Personally, I don't think that's a very plausible reason for getting a maid. Besides, I can't believe Lauren would actually say that with pride. But then she is white. In the black community it would be a crying shame to admit that your child's first word was '*Tata*', let alone that she called out to the maid first.

My other Girlfriend, Nosizwe, is on the point of convincing me, though. Her excuse for getting a maid, besides needing a nanny for her husband's bastard children, is the high unemployment rate. She says she's 'doing her bit, with her measly pay' for the economy. That lightens the load on my conscience.

This being the case, my boardroom mind is getting into gear and I am beginning to wonder if a maid's salary counts for tax breaks?

'Sorry, ma'am. SARS says you don't qualify for a tax break because you earn too much,' my long-suffering PA informs me.

'So how much would I have to earn to qualify?'

She laughs. 'Way below what you are used to.'

'Less than your pay?'

'Way less ... It seems you have to be in the three grand or less bracket,' she answers.

Sad that I don't qualify for tax breaks, but tragic that there are people in that income bracket who need maids. If my life was not such a busy one, I would run for presidential office on the ticket of 'Free Maids for the Working Poor' – paid for out of state coffers, of course.

So, now that I have surrendered and have seen the need for a maid, I need a plan of action.

There is a halfway house for reformed female convicts not far from my home. I have done some voluntary admin work over there and donate clothes whenever I update my wardrobe. It may be the only halfway house with ex-cons who dress in Prada, worn once, because Nosizwe – aka 'The Clothes Horse' – also donates there. I'm thinking of offering one of the 'inmates' a job. That way, I'll be getting the help I need while ensuring that an employably-challenged individual has an income, and my conscience will not be overburdened by *bourgeois* guilt.

In spite of my wish to assist in the reduction of unemployment, I am not going to hire a black woman. This is not so much because I do not believe in 'sister power', but because I have a short fuse. Should I bring my office personality home, I would feel less guilty lashing out at a white person than a black person. Racist, you want to call me. I probably am, but there is one in all of us. If you are going to be honest, how many times have you, in the comfort of your own race, made a generalised statement about someone of another race when they have failed to meet your exacting standards?

So I'm going to be honest and tell you that I simply do not have it in me to insult a 'sister' in my home and I do not have the patience to give criticism in a sensitive way, as our culture requires. Besides, it will be very interesting to note how Lauren, my 'liberal' white friend and neighbour, who has a black maid, will react to this. I am seeing this as a social experiment – and hoping it might assist Lauren to see her maid as a human being rather than one of 'those people' of which, apparently, Nosizwe and I are exceptions.

I pick up the phone and dial my husband's number.

'Babes? I am getting a maid.'

'That's good that you finally decided, hon. It will take a load off.'

'A white girl,' I whisper into the phone conspiratorially.

'Is this one of your little crusades to show Lauren how biased she is?' he laughs. The man knows me only too well.

'Never. I just think unemployed whites deserve as much of an opportunity as unemployed blacks. Call it White Economic Empowerment, if you will. But don't tell anyone, okay?'

'Okay, babes, I won't tell anyone. You do what you want about hiring your maid, but I have to go, there's a patient waiting for me.'

Huh. Men always whine about not being involved in household decisions, but listen to that man saying 'your' and not 'our' maid, as though she will be serving me alone.

I send an SMS to my father: *Thinking of getting a white maid*. He texts me back immediately: *Make sure she does the toilets*.

Before I go maid-recruiting though, I can tell you are dying to hear about Nosizwe and Lauren ...

CHAPTER 1

Nosizwe the Clothes Horse

Nosizwe does not work out, and eats whatever she wants. Although she was not blessed with the prettiest Xhosa face, she is one of the few who does not possess the Xhosa passport – otherwise known to all as the humongous butt. She does, however, possess a physique that is perfect in every way – pert breasts, well-toned ass, a waist that would make a wasp jealous, cellulite-free thighs, killer legs ... And as if that weren't enough advantage, Siz, as I call her, is one of those few black South African pre-independence children who were born with beaded silver spoons in their mouths.

Her father was a businessman and her mother a pretty, twenty-years-younger nurse, who saw an opportunity and grabbed it. Her dad already had children aplenty from one marriage and several flings, and was lucky to have been born and gone at a time when Aids was unknown. Such was the power of her mother's mojo that when Siz's father died when she was five, he stipulated that everything in his will belonged to this pretty young nurse, and had even set up an exclusive trust fund for Siz and her younger sister Nomalizwe, known to all as Lizwe. Not only did Siz's father leave a will at a time when few, if any, black people did so, but also in those days children born out of wedlock had no claim on the estate (to protect the many white children who had 'coloured' siblings?) so Siz, her mother, and her sister inherited the man's vast business interests as well. The first wife didn't contest the will because she was under-educated and therefore ignorant of the law and her children's rights. Besides, she would have had the fight of her life on her hands had she tried. 'Why?' you ask. You have to know Siz's mother to understand. She is one of those characters who, when she walks in and out of a room, leaves you feeling as though you have been through a powerful hurricane. Today, with her children out of the house and as a grand-mother to Lizwe's six-year-old son, her word is still law. Shit, her word is even law to Mandla, Lauren, Lauren's husband Michael, and I, and we are not even related to her.

But Siz's mother is not just a pretty face with hurricane mojo; she has brains and ambition to match and managed to turn a two-bit business in Langa into a chain of super-markets in the Eastern and Western Cape, while still main-taining great contacts with the then-banned South African political parties, without seeming like a sellout for having money. As if all that were not enough, her second marriage was to one of the leaders of the United Democratic Front who did a stint on 'the Isle'. With her business acumen and his political connections, Siz's mother became a 'must-know' post-1991. When Black Economic Empowerment came into play, all the honkies wanted to partner up with her. She now co-owns a bunch of companies, sits on numerous boards of directors, and is a multi-millionaire in her own right.

Unfortunately, as most people know, rich parents are either very generous or very stingy, and Siz's mother falls into the former category with her last born and the latter with her first born. Sure, she armed Siz with a preppie South

African private girls' school education to matric level, and a posh public school for A-Levels in the UK, and then an even more expensive private university in the States – specifically Hawaii, where Siz and I met. But she was strict on Siz, trust fund or not, and gave her a measly allowance every semester, allegedly to foster responsibility. 'After all, you are the first born. You are supposed to *learn* responsibility,' Siz would often mimic her mother after one of our drunken episodes on dollar-pitcher night at Moose's. I smile, as one can only do with a full belly, when I remember the times that girl and I lunched on stale hot dogs from 7–Eleven.

For my part, I could not help her much financially. I hated calling home to ask for funds; my father would tell me about some distant cousin he had just assisted financially in one way or another, and I would end up telling him, 'I was just calling to see how you are.' There we were in what the rest of the world considers a paradise, Hawaii, without two pennies to rub together. Paradise lost? Indeed.

It was different with her baby sister, Lizwe, though. Lizwe is clearly the apple of her mother's eye. She didn't have to work for all the seven years she spent doing her undergraduate at NYU. Lizwe, you see, could never make up her mind what she wanted to study, and so touched on Information Systems, Pre-Med and, eventually, when even her mother was getting fed up, got her degree in Business Studies.

When Nosizwe graduated and returned home, she begged and scraped to find employment but did not ask for help from her mother, not wanting to deal with any more emotional guilt about 'everything I've done for you'. Eventually she hooked an executive job with a French multinational company in Johannesburg. The way Siz tells it: 'My blackness was imperative and my intelligence apparently just an added advantage, so I am forever having to prove myself to those white boys in suits.' She now lives two blocks from me in Lombardy East because, I flatter myself, she needs me as an anchor in her dramatic life.

Although she is very judgmental (like her mother) with a strong sense of wrong and right, Siz has never been a very good judge of character when she likes someone. This may explain her marital union. I think homegirl watched too much *Soul Food* because, like Bird, she married an ex-con who her mother detests with a passion. I am sometimes a little unsure whether Siz has remained married to Vuyo because she is trying to 'show' her mother, or because he is one of the sweetest, funniest, most loving, most charming – and not to mention 'prettiest' – boys a woman could hope to catch.

He's also the only person we know who can stand up to Siz's mother. With his athletic physique, his zero-curse-word vocabulary and a teddy-bear personality, Vuyo can aptly be described as a Gentleman-Thug. He has a steady job – which is more than can be said for a lot of the black male population in South Africa. But there is a down side to Vuyo. Two of them, to be exact.

The first is that he came with the baggage of two ghetto-fabulous babymamas, who seem not to care that Vuyo is a married man now. The second is that Vuyo loves his two bastard sons and Siz is barren and so, unsurprisingly, she resents the brats.

Vuyo always had a way with ladies and prior to Siz coming into his life, had two simultaneous girlfriends from Zola in Soweto. They hated each other and, maybe each hoping they could get one over on the other, they both got pregnant. Both hoodrats had sons and, out of spite, both named their boys Vuyo.

Vuyo loves his boys, but unfortunately for the babymamas, this was not enough reason for him to marry either one of them. Not long after he and Siz got hitched, the ghetto-fabs dumped their brood on Siz's doorstep. Siz tolerates having Vuyo 2 and 3 around because, jealous chick that she is, she prefers to have her man home with her than visiting babymamas.

In spite of her issues, Siz has got to be one of the staunchest friends any person could have. She is one of those people who loves and hates with such passionate fervour that I feel lucky to be on the love side of her coin. This is not to say that we always agree. We had some big fights in college, which almost always began with her complaining about the guy she was dating. I, foolishly, would play my 'leave-him' Sis Dolly role and shake my head derisively when she did not. I now know not to give my opinions, because she will repeat them to her man, and when they are back in honeymoon mode they will end up blaming me for all their problems. I tell you, our friendship is working out much better because I am no longer a busybody.

Siz is a shopaholic and her wardrobe hangs like the who's who of Milan Fashion Week. This girl will travel to Paris just to buy clothes. She never takes heed when I tell her that clothes don't maketh the woman, my philosophy being, 'I don't walk around with the price tag out so why buy one outfit for four grand when I can buy twenty for the same amount at Mr Price?' I once asked her why she insists on going to London, Paris and New York to shop for designer wear when our homegrown Sun God'dess' are just as good? 'Girl please,' (insert eye-roll) 'until I hear Halle on Oscar's red carpet saying, "It's a Sun God'dess", I am not buying. I ply my trade back home and not overseas, that's all the Proudly South African I need. So you and your folks at Nedlac can continue with your local designers.'

Aside from her misguided clothes budget allocation, Siz is a very generous soul and is always giving. In fact, whenever she goes to Europe on a shopping stint, she makes sure she brings all of us something – she is the one who introduced me to my one designer weakness: my Mahnolos.

With her warm and giving nature, Siz recently made a gesture that is typically her by going home – 'home' to me and her being anywhere in the Eastern Cape – and taking some distant cousin from Zwelitsha, with no livelihood and three children, to come and live with her and help take care of her stepsons. Siz has actually taken time to enrol this distant cousin, Pertunia, in weekly sewing classes which she pays for. She drops Pertunia off and picks her up again on Saturdays, while she spends the day with the step-children whose existence she detests – a true sacrifice. Considering that Sisi Pertunia is a very distant relative – a relation by clan name only – this is really big of Siz.

Lauren asked her about this. 'Honestly Siz, doesn't getting a maid and training her for something better defeat the whole purpose of hiring help? Just when she is getting used to all your bad habits, she'll be telling you she is leaving. Hello!'

I am in agreement with Lauren on this but Siz was not buying it. She merely put her palm in our faces and said, 'Y'all talk to the white 'cause this black ain't listening.'

This social consciousness is admirable, but even her mother, 'Madam Negativity', told her she was going to regret it, because 'darkies always bite the hand that feeds them'. Nosizwe responded that so long as those darkies' stomachs were full, she was happy. (But she said it to me – saying it to her mother would result in one of those meaningless curses that affect one's psyche so much that any time anything goes wrong you assume it is because of *the curse*.)

Finally, Nosizwe is my son's official godmother. While

neither Mandla nor I are religious, we were both raised by staunch Catholic mothers. It happened then that one day, about a month after Hintsa was born, I took him to visit his doting grandmother in Soweto. She summoned me into the living room, sat me down and, in the manner of mothers-in-law who have something serious to talk about, asked me when was the last time I attended church.

Now, I havn't been to church since I was sixteen. Mandla and I got married at a registry office and we both still avoid funerals due to our aversion to organised religion. So I found myself lying that it was a few weeks ago. She smiled the smile of mothers-in-law who know you are lying but plan to just let it pass, and bluntly ordered me to get the child baptised.

This meant having to attend mass regularly and paying church dues so Mandla and I could seem like devout members of the congregation. But I did not mind as much as I thought I would; Mandla and I saw the positive side of the whole thing in two words: Catholic education. Having both benefited from it, we agreed that a Catholic education is probably the greatest weapon you can arm a child with, in spite of the bad rap that the good Church has taken in recent years.

This being the case, the boy was baptised. Siz was made godmother and that was the last time either Mandla, Hintsa's godmother or I set foot in a church. When the priest asked us to affirm our faith by vowing to raise the child as a Catholic and promising to 'conquer Satan and all his works' we all felt no guilt in saying 'aye'. I suppose, should guilt nag us in our golden years, we will all go to confession and say so many Hail Marys. Siz being godmother to my son means nothing more to her or Hintsa than that she buys him a present every time she makes a business trip to France. But that's between Siz and her godson.

CHAPTER 2

Rule Brittania

If Nosizwe was born with a beaded silver spoon, Lauren was born with a wooden one. Her father, old imperial British stock, inherited a Stellenbosch vineyard and within five years of his marriage to Lauren's mother had drunk the profits away and mismanaged the farm so spectacularly that they had to sell it to a *nouveau riche* Afrikaner.

Not wanting to put a white man out to pasture (and maybe to push some Boer-English buttons while doing it), the Afrikaner farmer gave Lauren's father a managerial position on the farm which had originally belonged to him, and Lauren grew up as an Anglo *plaasmeisie,* without the *plaas.* Her mother had, apparently, never forgiven her father for pitching them into poverty and Lauren grew up with a mother who whined about how things could have been and a father who would drink too much and then beat her mother up. Ostensibly for 'blaming him' for their unfortunate position.

Lauren went to school with the farmer's children and when she finished high school, she got a scholarship to Wits and never looked back.

'You know Thandi, when I left Stellenbosch I told myself I would never go back there,' she once confided, 'I wouldn't even go to my father's funeral if he died. The man is a bastard. I don't only hate him for the way he drinks and beats my mother; I can't get over the fact that he drank away my trust fund and I had to apply for a scholarship to university.'

It could be a sign of her Electra Complex (thank you Dr Freud – although why she should want to possess her father is beyond me) that Lauren ended up marrying a man who also tends to drink a little too much. Fortunately for Lauren, her husband Michael is a lamb. Save for moments of possessiveness and ordering her about when he is drunk, he's a needy child to Lauren's big mama character.

When I first got to know her, Lauren told me that to escape the abuse drama, her mother would often reminisce about how British royal blood coursed through their veins – whatever colour that was in *that* inbred monarchy. Thus began Lauren's love affair with The Royal Family and royal memorabilia. A love affair she now shares with another royalist who acts like she came from African aristocratic stock – Siz's mother.

As if her Anglophilia were not laughable enough, Lauren has to make it more comical. Just last week she was bragging to Siz and me that she had enrolled her eldest daughter, Elizabeth (yes, named after the other more famous Liz), in a Sotho class. Siz and I were baffled.

'Maybe this is Lauren's attempt at White Cultural Empowerment,' Siz suggested. 'If the whites know what the natives are saying then they can stay ahead of the BEE boat.'

'It's always about black and white with you two isn't it?' sneered Lauren. 'As a matter of fact, I enrolled her because Prince Harry is always going to Lesotho and, who knows … she is almost a teenager. If she speaks Sotho well enough, being a translator could just be her way back to our royal roots.'

Siz and I gawped. This was even better than WCE. That

said, nothing is ever black and white in this country and as much as Lauren brags about her aristocratic background, she is equally touchy about her Africanness. She is constantly trying to 'prove' how we are all immigrants to South Africa, and so are all equally African. This normally leads to amusing run-ins between her and Siz.

Nosizwe argues that in all the forms issued at all the post-apartheid institutions she has visited, she has always seen 'race' followed by African, Coloured, White or Asian. If whites are Africans, as the apartheid regime liked to insist, why aren't they making as much noise about the racial classification on institutional forms as they are about Afrikaans language usage in public institutions or Black Economic Empowerment? At this point, Lauren usually gets stumped and takes it as a cue to launch an anti-Mugabe rant. Interestingly, she has never been to Zimbabwe.

An English lecturer at Wits University, Lauren loves knowledge and children. In no particular order. Therefore it should come as no surprise when I tell you that, at thirty-two, Lauren is still studying – this time for her doctorate in English Literature. She has also been breeding since she and Michael got married immediately after she got her BA at the age of twenty-one. With four biological children and hundreds of university students, Lauren rarely dresses up and is perpetually kitted out in khakis and one of Michael's shirts.

Although she loves children, I do not quite understand why Lauren had four of her own. When she is reading a good book (which is more often than you know), she shuns motherly responsibility entirely and gives the children to her maid, MaRosie. This may explain why the last two enunciated 'Rosie' before they could say Mama. 'When they are good, they are mine,' she likes to joke. 'When they are noisy, they are MaRosie's.'

Lauren and I met when my family moved in next door. Realising I had no sugar for that refreshing cup of tea one simply must have after unpacking, and noting that I was surrounded by white people in my new home, I tentatively rang her gate bell. She seemed the less intimidating and more liberal of my two neighbours. I had judged correctly. She and Mike invited us in and Mike and Mandla were soon sharing a six-pack while my son, Hintsa, had quickly become 'just like a brother' to Junior, Elizabeth, Charles and Diana. Lauren and I got along like a house on fire and in no time she became the third member of the Awesome Twosome that Siz and I had been.

Lauren has one major flaw, though … and that is her inherent racism. She does not notice it, or chooses to say she doesn't, but Siz and I can tell from the way she treats her maid. You would think a progressive someone in a progressive institute of higher learning would not have the hang-ups of other white surburbanites, but nope. She tells Siz and me 'I love everyone'. She always gives money to begging white alcoholics holding placards at the traffic lights reading: 'Four children, all unemployed because of BEE; wife dead; farm taken by Mugabe's government,' but she treats simple, hard-working, poor, black folk with suspicion. I recall one time a pair of her shoes went missing and she was on the brink of firing Rosie when she found them on the back seat of her car. You would think, of course, that since MaRosie is so good with her children she would respect her as an equal, but sadly no … and this bothers me.

Because Lauren is my neighbour I, more than Siz or anyone else, see the treatment she metes out to MaRosie. It's a source of constant annoyance to see someone older than my mother treated with so much contempt by someone who, by the grace of heavens, is neither of her race nor her child. Poor Rosie, who Lauren considers 'part of the family' (a poor relation maybe?) has to wake up at four-thirty to iron everybody's clothes before they go to work or school because Lauren always insists that clothes should be 'freshly pressed'. Rosie then has to make breakfast. Even in these days of fortified cereals, Lauren insists on Rosie making a full English every day of the week. 'You know breakfast is the most important meal of the day,' Lauren justifies when I question her about this interesting habit. No wonder Lauren and her babies are all a little horizontally-gifted.

Because of Lauren's size, I enjoy going shopping with her because, for once, I can have a bigger female friend to ask: 'Do I look fat in this?' even when I know I look damn good. I have often thought that maybe Lauren treats MaRosie the way she does so that she can feel good about herself. 'I am white. I have a good job. I PAY you. Get it together,' seems to be her attitude.

But when I see the relationship that Lauren has with Ma, I wonder whether she really is a racist, or whether I am just racially sensitive. Maybe she is just 'classist'? Lauren and Siz's mother burn the phone lines between East London and Johannesburg, for no apparent reason other than to confide about the latest royal scandal or royal outfit. In our private conversations, Siz and I often imitate them.

Siz as Ma: 'You won't believe this ... I just found out that Queen Elizabeth and I share not only the same dislike for people who act in a common way, but also the same birthday.'

Me as Lauren: 'I *know*. I forgot to tell you that when I was reading the official biography I noted that she was also born on the twenty-first of April. That's probably why you are such a strong person, Ma ... and very colour-coordinated, just like the Queen. Although, I must say, even when you reach her age I think you will still be looking better than her. You do know we're actually related? My mother's cousin was married to the Queen's second cousin twice removed.'

Siz as Ma: 'Of course my darling, but back to me. My girl, you know God didn't fault me in the looks department. In fact, maybe we should try to see the Queen and give her some fashion advice. I think you and I should go to the Chelsea Flower Show next month.'

Me as Lauren: 'I was just thinking about that. There might be some Americans there who we can teach a thing or two about *culture*.'

Siz as Ma: 'Truly, my child. You are right. You are always right darling. And a True Leo. Why can't Nosizwe and Thandi be more like you?'

Siz and I have nicknamed Lauren and Mama 'OBE's' – Odious Babes of the Empire.

CHAPTER 3

And Then There is Me

And then there is me. I like to think I was given the name Thandi because of the great love that I know my parents had for each other. I am neither silver-spoon nor wooden-spoon born, but an average South African – although both Siz and Lauren claim they are more South African than I will ever be and that, with my immense global experience, I am far from being average. (Although, when I describe myself as an 'average South African', I am talking of South Africa being a middle-income country, developmentally speaking, and yours truly being a middle-class person; which makes me an average citizen.) But, having dished the dirt on my friends, I will tell you the biased version of my own story. It goes like this:

My father and my mother would be referred to as 'col-oureds' (whatever colour that is) during the apartheid era, and even today in South Africa's post-apartheid days. They were both politically active, joining the African National Congress and border-jumping at a time when other so-called 'coloureds' were just grateful that, in spite of the hardships of the apartheid regime, they still had it better than the (to use the terminology of that dark shadow in our nation's history) 'kaffirs'.

My father left South Africa in 1970 to join *Umkhonto we Sizwe* in Tanzania and that is where he met my mother. I was born in Dar es Salaam, where my father was undergoing military training and my mother had every woman's dream job (at that time), the highly-esteemed role of typist.

My paternal grandfather was a Scotsman who had an affair with his former maid, my grandmother. The result of this union was my father. I grew up with an aversion towards white men as my father had told me that my grandmother was raped.

Whether it was that my father read too many Malcolm X speeches or simply a sign of the times in which he grew up, my father tended to exaggerate. It was only when I came back home as a young adult that I realised that my *Makhulu* could never have been raped. Her boss was definitely guilty of sexual exploitation, but the grandmother I knew, who spoke her mind to one and all, would never have been forced into sex. Even the white sergeants at Orlando Police Station knew not to mess with her.

My take on it, after knowing her, is that perhaps she thought she would be able to do a *coup d'etat* on the Missus but when the Missus found out, she got fired and became a liquor trader on the alternative market (also known as the black market!) which is how she put my father through school. If my father wants to justify the fact that he is strongly anti-white by stating that his mother was raped, I let him be. (What surprises me is that he chose the ANC as a political home, as opposed to the blacker and, back then, more militant Pan-Africanist Congress.)

It may have been to fit in with his comrades that my father used his mother's last name, acted blacker than the blackest, and instilled in me the same values. One thing I applaud my father for is that he has never (as a few other so-called 'coloureds' have done) claimed to have Khoisan heritage in order to take advantage of the special allowances reserved for those very indigenous people. He states that the Khoisan are disadvantaged enough without him having to jump on the bandwagon. He is just a black man – and he speaks all the local languages as though he was born and bred in every province of this great country.

Unlike my father, my mother never lied about her heritage. She told me her grandfather was an Englishman who came to South Africa, met a good-time girl in my grandmother (she was a singer), and shagged her to prove that he was liberal (and maybe deep down inside, to see whether it was true what they said about black women and their sexuality).

Of course there had never been a chance that he would marry her but after he left, with promises to return, my grandmother didn't ever have any serious relationships. Thus she was detested by many men in Kofifi for thinking she was too good for them. Without their support, her music career went nowhere but, like many women before and after her, she kept on singing 'Waiting for my man'.

He never came back, and she died a solitary figure in Soweto's Orlando West after the resettlement. My mother's self-imposed exile was, therefore, less for political reasons than that she hoped for better opportunities and had nothing to stay in South Africa for.

She met my father in Tanzania and I like to think that it was love at first sight because my parents' relationship is what I strive for in my marriage to Mandla. My late mother told me they had hoped to have a brood of children, but after she gave birth to me, three miscarriages and doctor's warnings made it such that I was an only child. I am not complaining. While it is true that I did not get everything I wanted, I sure did get everything I needed and, in retrospect, I could not have asked for anything more.

Although my parents loved me deeply, I was always on the periphery of their love for each other and, without meaning to I am sure, sometimes they made me feel like 'the other' in the equation that was our family. When my father came home – wherever home was at the time – he'd put a Temptations album on the record player and start singing 'My Girl' to my mother, like she was the only girl in the room.

It used to make me lonely, but it was also a testament to their love, how they would waltz together as though they were one, and how at parties they only had eyes for each other. My father and mother had an unspoken language; they knew what the other wanted to say before it was said just by looking into each other's eyes. If they fought, I am sure it occurred only in their bedroom because I never saw them exchanging angry words.

When I was twelve, my parents sent me to high school in the United Kingdom courtesy of the liberation movement. Thus began my love-hate relationship with that little island with a population whose teeth were so messed up prior to the National Health Service that many of them looked as though they grew up on a diet of snoek. I was in boarding school but spent many holidays with numerous exile aunts and uncles while my parents pursued the liberation cause.

My very first experience of 'home', therefore, occurred only after the unbanning of the political parties. Fortunately for me, my parents had educated me enough to cherish my culture and I spoke Xhosa relatively well. Granted, it was with a bit of an English lilt, but in those days of a xenophobic pre-independence black populace, excusing my accent as the result of a life in exile guaranteed that I got the cutest boys, and that my friends' parents made allowances for misdeeds that in an 'in-zile' would have been considered a no-no.

After putting the ANC in power with my vote, I buried my mother who died of cancer. Her daughter and husband were drawn closer by their shared sorrow; I became the best friend that my mother had been to him and he became the confidante that his wife had been to me.

I cried a few tears of blood to get my father to allow me to study in Hawaii and, never having been the father who could say no to his perfect child, he consented. When he enquired why I wanted to go to Hawaii I lied, straight faced, that I was curious to learn about the culture and history of its indigenous people. The truth of the matter was that the land of the *Kanaka Maolis*, *poi* and *ka'awa* was the sole place where I knew that my father did not have any eyes and ears, and that made it FREEDOMLAND.

Just before my senior year, while on summer vacation in New York, I met Mandla at a party at Lizwe's Manhattan flat. He had driven all the way from DC to attend the party with a few other South African gatecrashers, but all of us were homesick and any South African passport was welcome.

The world did not stop turning, there were no sparks in the air, images did not start moving in slow motion; rather we chatted for a bit, exchanged numbers and became friends. We talked regularly and when we returned home, I suppose for lack of choice – I jest! – Mandla and I gravitated towards each other and here we are, seven years later with a five-year-old son and a six-year-old marriage.

When Mandla proposed, there was no picnic basket in the park, no jet flying overhead scripting, 'Thandile, will you marry me?' It was more a realisation as we loaded the trunk of his car after a joint grocery-shopping excursion that moving from one apartment to another each week was getting ridiculous. As he got into the car he said to me, 'Babes, buying the same groceries for two places is absurd, why don't we just get married?' Sure, it was hardly romantic, but I said yes. After all, Mandla was intelligent, he had a great career ahead of him, he loved me and he was a great shag. So he needed a little help in the romance department, but I had a whole lifetime to work on that. And I flatter myself that I was not a bad catch for him either, otherwise he would not have wanted to, as they say, 'buy the restaurant when he was getting free meals'.

Those who know me refer to me as black, because that is what I am. But many who do not know me refer to me, maybe due to my caramel complexion and none-too-fro Afro, as coloured. I honestly hate the term and I recall getting into a bit of conflict with another so-called coloured who told me I did not have pride in my heritage. Now with all due respect, I cannot very well celebrate my European ancestors who never loved enough to acknowledge their offspring. My African ancestors, on the other hand, have always loved unstintingly and supported unconditionally, so why celebrate those who did not love? Besides, anyone who has travelled knows if 'you got a drop of black blood, you's just a nigger and you suffers from the same prejudices and mistreatment all the other niggers be getting'.

But maybe Siz is right. Maybe sometimes I tend to overcompensate in order to fit in, just as other 'bi-racial' (as the Brits like to call us) children tend to do in order to be welcome by our darker kinsfolk. I mean, just a look at history is enough to highlight this. Malcolm X was bi-racial (his grandfather, like mine, was white) and he detested white people with a passion. Bob Marley wrote many controversial songs directed at his white ancestors.

Somehow it is always the blackness that is celebrated. Is it possible that the black ancestral blood running through their veins comes back to haunt white people through the cultural loss of their children? (Of course if this is the case, the black South African ancestors, apart from my parents and a few others, have remained rather passive in this respect.)

Perhaps I am seeking revenge for my black ancestors by doing the white maid thing? Granted, since I will be paying her more than the minimum labour allowance set by the Domestic Workers' Union it's more like fair employment than revenge, but I cannot help feeling some sort of glee in the darkest chamber of my dark heart that yearns to yell at middle-income white people with black maids: 'We are all equal after all, you got a black maid and I have a white one!'

CHAPTER 4

The Recruitment

It's May. The rain has stopped and one can now see the dead leaves. I hate autumn with its browning grass, shedding of leaves and the uncertainty of whether it's going to be an acceptable winter or a freezing winter – freezing to me being anything below twenty degrees centigrade.

It has been two months since I resolved to get myself a maid and I have not yet done so, because I have been too busy during the week, and too lethargic during the weekends, but I cannot do all the housework alone anymore so today is the day. Besides, I have done my seasonal wardrobe upgrade and there is no space for the extra clothes, so going to the halfway house will therefore serve two purposes. Vuyo is taking his sons to see his family in Soweto today and Siz, who has also done her wardrobe clearance, is coming to pick me up.

I hope Marita is still there. She's a sweet Afrikaans girl from Kroonstad I've talked to the few times that I have gone to do voluntary bookkeeping at the halfway house. She is funny, seems quite intelligent, and from my few conversations with her she is 'right on' in her approach to life. And of course, she is white.

Siz arrives wearing a BabyPhat tight tank top in pink, a pair of BabyPhat blue jeans and some pink Pumas. Her casual look is so well pulled-off that she looks as though she is in her very early twenties and would make many in that demographic jealous. More importantly, she is making me feel dowdy in my coffee and cream khakis and tee. Dammit, I am really beginning to feel as though 'my butt looks big in this', but it wouldn't look too good if I went to change, so I just get on with it.

'Hey girl, looking good,' I say to her.

'You don't look like the mother of a five-year-old, so pretty good yourself,' she responds. It's not really a compliment but I dutifully give the prerequisite Continental European three kisses for intimates. I'm still not used to kissing people on the lips, à la most South Africans – it feels too much like a violation. With Mandla's mother, it even begins to feel like incestuous lesbianism. Eeuw!

Siz and Mandla are the only ones who have been apprised of what is about to happen, and with this in mind she says, 'I can't wait to see the look on Lauren's face when she gets hold of the situation.'

'Girl, just chill. You know what Lauren's like so if I get the white girl, please be cool about it and act like it's the most normal thing in the world,' I say.

She responds with a laugh, 'But it isn't, is it? Boy, I love South Africa. Only here can you think of baiting your white friend by getting a white maid, while all your sisters in England have white babysitters.'

As usual Siz's boot and passenger seats are filled to the brim with all the clothes she purchased in Paris on multiple business trips – clothes she thought she was going to wear, but never got around to. Talk about a shopaholic. I am therefore going to have to take the Bond-machine , my metallic grey Aston Martin. I ask my son, who by now is having a very intense conversation with his godmother, 'Babes, do you want to come with mommy and Aunt Siz or do you want to stay with daddy?' I want Hintsa to come with us, to make sure that Marita, or whoever I get, is good with children.

Sensing he is about to say no so he can stay on the Play-station with his dad I add a bribe: 'Afterwards we can all go for ice creams.' Forget my figure. I only live once, right?

The ice cream wins him over, but he insists on riding with Aunt Siz. That means I get a chance to drive by myself and look like a cool, successful, single chick, so I agree.

'Make sure you look at the road and if anyone ogles you at the traffic lights, put up your left hand and tell them you are happily married to the man who bought that expensive piece of jewellery.' Mandla has just come to the door and says this to me as he kisses Siz hello/bye.

Yeah, whatever. I feel like I have 'married' tattooed on my forehead, and if anyone ogles it's going to be at the car and not at wifely, mommy, think-my-waist-is-getting-too-thick Thandi. I put the top down and start fantasising about the first time I introduce my new maid to Lauren.

Marita's story is a sad one. She's from one of those few poor Afrikaner families who failed to take advantage of apartheid's provisions; a girl who grew up in a caravan park with her ma, pa, oupa and ouma, four brothers and three sisters. She felt privileged when some biker boy from Johannesburg came by, swept her off her feet and whisked her away at full throttle to what she thought would be a great adventure in Joburg.

Alas, they had different expectations. He had hoped to get a *mevrou* to install in his rundown Hillbrow studio flat who would love, obey, honour and constantly get him money for alcohol through the oldest trade known to womankind, while doing his washing and cooking his food in her non-business hours. But that wasn't all. This oke started beating on her every time she didn't make as much cash as he expected. One day, when his Boere ancestors were evidently not with him, Marita got fed up with being beaten, took the revolver he used to threaten her with, and blew his brains out.

She was given a life sentence but the New National Order (read: post-apartheid government) worked it such that she was paroled, and now she is at the halfway home awaiting permanent employment and a fixed address. She has since been forever grateful to the NNO, and I am sure she will be relieved at getting a job offer, regardless of who offers it, because she has already been there for a year.

Siz and her godson pull up in her black C200 and park next to me when we arrive. I get out and pull my T-shirt down over my khakis. Shit, I really need to lose weight.

After two trips to my car and what seems like ten to Siz's, we finally have everything. By this time the girls at the House have gathered around us in the visitors' lounge and are admiring the clothes in the boxes. Marita is one of them. Thank God, she was still here.

We exchanged pleasantries and I quickly decided to go and talk to the coordinator. I left Siz with Hintsa, knowing that she might titter or make some sarcastic comment, which would result in my not getting the girl of my choice.

I knock on the coordinator's door and, after the niceties, I get straight into it because I always find it tough beating about the bush.

'I've been talking to one of your ladies since I started coming here and I was wondering, would it be a big loss on your part if I borrowed her to help me out?' I said.

She smiled ever-so-sweetly, probably welcoming the opportunity to have another ex-con off her hands, and asked me which one I had in mind. 'Marita,' I responded, quickly adding, before she said no, 'I am also very keen for my son to learn what I feel is an important South African language. Unfortunately my Afrikaans knowledge is dismal at best. Marita is the best speaker of that language I have come across – apart from yourself of course,' I ended, with a flourish. Obviously I had pressed the right button because the coordinator's face, which had become rather pinched when I mentioned Marita's name, lit up. 'What exactly would she be doing?' she asked.

Knowing the sensitivities of South African society, new South African or not, and knowing equally well that I would never be allowed to cross the line of having a white woman for a maid, I deliberately fudged, 'I know that she has been doing some sewing and I have a cottage where she can do that and perhaps market her clothes. In return she could also help me, in her free time, to pick my son up from school and tutor him Afrikaans and his other homework.'

The coordinator seemed to like the idea. 'We just need to ask Marita,' she said, sending someone to call her.

When Marita came in the coordinator said sternly, 'Marita. This lady wants you to come and help tutor her son in Afrikaans while you are staying with her. How do you feel about that?' So she was primarily a tutor now. But I was not going to make corrections and I knew I had it in the bag when Marita said, in her thick Afrikaans accent, 'Really? I can come and stay with you? Oh thank you so much madam. Thank you, thank you.' *She had called me madam!* The only people who call me 'madam' are Mandla's friends and they say it in a denigrating way. I thought, 'I like this girl. Yeah. I could definitely work with her!'

With the deal done, I walked out with Marita, who was still calling me madam, to Siz and Hintsa. 'She sure knows her place – Lauren would like her too,' Siz whispered to me as I got close to her. I nudged her and muttered, 'Shuddup ...'

Marita may have called me 'madam' but her job was not secure yet. I had to make sure she got on with the 'prince', who would be doing most of the interaction with her. I introduced them, and Hintsa smiled at her shyly. She managed to coax him into a conversation, and soon they were having an intense discussion about what happened in the last episode of *DragonBallZ*.

Away from the coordinator, I explained that she would have her own cottage, furnished with a bed, pots, plates, fridge and stove, and that she would have to help me out with hanging the laundry and ironing and cleaning the house, in addition to taking Hintsa back and forth to nursery school. 'Is that okay?' I asked, searching her face for signs of protest to my generosity. Instead, what I saw was a face that lit up with delight.

'It is. It is, and thank you for thinking of me,' she answered with enthusiasm.

'But aren't you going to have a problem with people referring to you as a maid for kaffirs?' I asked, wanting to get it out of the way.

Marita flinched visibly when I used the k-word and said, 'Sorry madam, please don't use words like that around me, *ne*?' It was obvious she was being genuine. 'The only people who have been really good to me are black people. I even voted for the ANC in the last election and would have done the same in the last two elections if I hadn't been in prison.' Siz, who was watching from the sidelines, playing with Hintsa and pretending not to pay attention, laughed.

Siz knows how I dislike it when white people try too

hard to show that they are liberal; I find it insincere. How did Marita even know I was pro-ANC since we had never talked politics? (Although it would be difficult to find any middle-class black person who is strongly anti-ANC at this moment in time.)

What the heck though, at least I would have a maid who had passed Standard Nine, had passable English and would be able to read Hintsa *Aesop's Fables* when I stayed late at the office. She would also be able to help him with his alphabet and other little pre-school homeworks. And since my knowledge of Afrikaans was, as I had told the coordinator, almost non-existent, she would definitely be handy to have around should Afrikaans become one of the eleven official languages the little man wants to learn. 'Okay then. Consider yourself hired,' I told her.

I arranged to come and pick Marita up the following Saturday. This would, hopefully, give her sufficient time to pack.

'*Ag,* sorry to bother you madam, but I don't have any bags,' Marita said meekly. 'Can you *mos* lend me some?'

Here was my chance to get my future maid to think I was the greatest person on earth, while getting Mandla to think I had actually consulted him on a ready-made decision about the maid. 'I can do better than that,' I told her. 'I'll go buy some and my husband will bring them to you tomorrow, is that all right?'

'*Baie dankie*, madam. Oh thank you so much,' she gushed.

Hintsa, Siz and I immediately made tracks to Eastgate to test the power of plastic. By mid-afternoon, we had amassed loads of bags full of shoes and the little man was complaining that he was tired. 'That's why I never want to come with you and Aunt Siz, mommy!' They grow up so fast these children – now when did this boy learn to talk in absolutes?

'How dare you say *never* to your mummy, boy?' I playfully spanked his bum.

Siz smiled and said I should celebrate the joys of motherhood. Hers was a sad, longing, smile. I knew she wanted children judging from the way she spoilt her godson, nephew, and Lauren's children – not to mention the Vuyos 2 and 3, who she didn't even like – but the gods had not been so kind to her. And the mothers of her stepchildren showed her absolutely no respect or gratitude for all she was doing for their offspring.

Munchies led us to Ocean Basket because I was craving mussels. 'Girl you know I hate all that pretentious black people eating seafood crap, but just this once, since we are celebrating your madamhood, I will put up with it.' Unlike me, Siz is seriously lacking in adventure as far as food is concerned. If it's not beef, chicken or fish, she ain't having it. The food was good, the wine was better and the conversation was, as usual, highly controversial. I think Siz and I probably talk too much politics because more than once Hintsa has chipped in with his little opinion about the land question, white people or BEE, and I know it was not really a five-year old's opinion but something he had overheard. Siz was, naturally, impressed, 'I wish the junior Vuyos could be more like your boy.'

'Nu-uh. Siz, I think we are talking too much politics around this boy. I don't want him expelled from pre-school for airing our prejudices. Besides, Hintsa would probably be more subdued if he had an evil stepmother like you,' I teased.

I called Mandla to check in. 'Whatcha doing?' I asked.

'Some boys from Soweto just dropped by and we're having a few beers. Can you grab us some food, babes?'

Now I was not too anxious to get home. Unfortunately, Siz had to leave and I could not stay at the mall indefinitely, so I suggested to Hintsa that we go video-shopping at Game and thereafter lock ourselves in mommy and daddy's room with home-made buttered popcorn, liquorice and juice and watch some great cartoons.

As we walk to the parking lot my son looks up at me and tugs my hand.

'You know the nursery rhymes that I have at school?' I nod. He continues, 'Well, I have been thinking, if Jack Sprat's wife ate no lean, and Jack Sprat ate no fat, that would mean they did not eat well, right?'

'Yes baby. I am sure Jack Sprat and his wife did not have a balanced diet.' I laughed to myself: is the child a future psychiatrist or philosopher, or maybe just a really insightful head of state?

'Does this mean that Jack was really skinny and his wife was really fat?' he asks.

'Sweetie, it's rude to say skinny and fat. You are supposed to say a little overweight and a little underweight.' Why do I preach the kind of political correctness I do not exercise?

'So, are they like Auntie Lauren and Uncle Mike?'

I cannot laugh, but I tell myself that I'll save it to tell Siz. Meanwhile, I have to protect my friend's honour and her weight from my TV-addled, perfect-looking-cartoon-chicks-watching son.

'You see baby, Jack Sprat and his wife are not real people. They are made up and they did not eat right. You know Auntie Lauren and Uncle Mike eat right because you eat at their house all the time, so you cannot compare them to Jack Sprat and his wife,' I lecture.

On our way home, I drove to Ivory Park and picked up some braaied meat for the drunks, along with some pap and atchar, to ensure they would not interrupt Hintsa and my video session.

On arriving home Mandla, aka daddy, and his friends Nathi and What's-his-face were drunk as skunks. How could that be possible in the few hours that we had been away? And they kept drinking.

'Daddy, mommy was telling Auntie Siz that you would be drunk when we got home. Are you drunk?' my big-mouthed son asked.

His drunken father responded, 'Boy, I told you not to pay attention to the senseless words of women. Of course I am not drunk. Real men can handle their alcohol.' He was rewarded with a withering look from me which seemed to penetrate his drunken mind because he apologised. Mandla knew I hated it when he made sexist statements, particularly in the presence of our son – I wanted to raise a man who respected and cherished women.

In a huff, I took Hintsa into our room and locked the door. Thank God our bedroom has a fridge (for 'mommy and daddy' reasons I will not go into right now), an entertainment centre and an en suite bathroom. The drunken men were really annoying, but the plus side was that I got time to bond with this boy via something we both love greatly: watching *Shrek* and *Antz*. Hintsa fell asleep during the second movie so I carried him to his room and tucked him in.

Fortunately the guys decided not to sleep on the floor of my living room. It appears Mandla and his pals had yet another of their drunken fights, which normally result in mental kisses and all being forgotten next time they see each other. The good news for me was that there was only one semi-drunk fool I would have to make breakfast for the next morning. The bad news, alas, was that I was regaled with, 'I don't want to deal with these miscreants anymore. Let them eff off. They just want to mooch from me…' This, in typical drunken Mandla fashion, would go on until he fell asleep – because, should I nod off first, he would keep on waking me up to ask me what I thought and giving me sloppy, beer-soaked kisses.

When I woke up, I knew why the man said he was easy like a Sunday morning. Sunday is such a laid-back day – if it weren't for the rugrat who was knocking on his parents' door asking whether he could go next door to play with Lauren's kids. There was always more than enough food at Lauren's house, but I called Lauren anyway to warn her that my 'little Hoover' would be there in a mo. The kids were going to swim, and I would warm up the grill later on so Lauren, Mike, Siz, Vuyo and the kids could join us for a braai – after Mandla had completed his errand of taking the bags to Marita.

I played the sweet housewife and brought Mandla breakfast in bed (a ham and mushroom omelette, his regular five slices of bread and a Hansa). You could see the fool was hung over by the way he was squinting at the sun streaming through the windows after I cruelly opened the curtains. He could not help being sweet, though.

'Thanks for breakfast babes. I really needed the Hansa.' He paused. 'By the way, where is the boy?' I told him he was next door, then he winked that knowing, leering, post-drunken wink and said he would break his food fast after he had his soul food – I knew he meant me and I smiled flirtatiously, 'It can certainly be arranged, my dear husband, as soon as you run an errand to Marita and play your host role perfectly when the gang comes for a braai.'

You would think that would be a passion killer, but for this man anticipation seems to work up his appetite even more and for that I say 'yeah!'

Mandla had called Vuyo to come along with him. I asked Mandla what they thought of Marita and he said she seemed enthusiastic and appeared as if she would make an alright maid ('alright' being the greatest compliment that comes out of Mandla's mouth, unless he wants something or he is writing a best man's speech). He and Vuyo did not tell Mike about Marita as we still wanted to surprise Lauren. Apparently Vuyo was drooling – told Mandla that one cannot have chocolate ice-cream every day and in fact, a man's life called for a bit of vanilla.

The whole gang arrived in the afternoon. The men were busy with their beers and the grill, the kids were paddling in the pool and, while we sipped our wine and made the salad, I was counting the minutes until Lauren and Siz got into a confrontation. I just hoped that Siz would not mention my bloody maid to Lauren during one of her 'we are better than you' moments. Fortunately she was not in a baiting mood and it all went rather pleasantly.

It had been a highly laid-back, if momentous, weekend and a great way to begin a new week. One in which I would no doubt have to deal with the psychotic, lazy, 'I-don't-know-who-the-fuck-you-were-sleeping-with-to-get-the-post' deputy I reported to. This guy was the reason why, even when there was little actual work on the office front, I ended up getting home exhausted. I seem to spend most of my time clearing up his mess. I guess that's why The Woman always says, 'The best man for the job is a *wo*man.'

CHAPTER 5

Madamhood

The week after the braai was a strenuous one on the work front and I, for one, happily mouthed, 'thank God it's Friday' at five o'clock, and meant every word. My body craved a nice, long, luxurious, bubble-filled, candlelit soak in the bath. Unfortunately, this was not to be. One of the inflexible family rules, as sacred as family dinner three times a week, is that Friday is family fun night where we go bowling, or to the movies or some such 'bonding' activity. I suppose, since I insisted on it in the first place, I have to live up to the whole shebang.

On this particular Friday, Mandla was the one who had prepared our schedule so I waited to hear what The Man had in store. Actually, I knew that he had plotted to dump Hintsa at Siz's house for a sleepover after the family bonding, while the four of us went partying till the break o' dawn. I knew this because Siz had called me straight after he called her and told me so. 'But you aren't supposed to know, so act surprised.' I could do that.

When I got home, Mandla told me he had bought three tickets for the six-thirty show of *Shrek 2*. 'Babes, do you think we can pack an overnight bag for your son?' There was a twinkle in his eye. 'He's going for a sleepover.'

I responded with mock fury, 'Why the hell should I pack a bag when you decided on a sleepover for him without consulting his mother?'

'That's easy enough,' he responded, patting my bum. 'You know how you are always nagging that you and I don't ever do anything together any more? Well, I arranged it with Siz and Vuyo so we can have an Adult Night Out.'

'That is so sweet, babes!' If I do say so myself, I think I pulled off a performance worthy of an Oscar because Mandla leant over and kissed me to 'seal the deal'.

Wearing my little black dress that showed my assets to best advantage, with my smart-looking babydaddy and my son in his BabyGap jeans and sweatshirt compliments of his godmother, we moved on out to the Eastside, better known as Eastgate Mall.

The movie was crap. Right at the end, a few minutes before Shrek and his fellow cast members finished singing the karaoke, Mandla's son started pulling at his father and whispering none-too-quietly, 'Daddy, I need to go to the loo ...'

'Okay boy, let's roll,' his father said, getting up. My guess was that he was equally unimpressed with *Shrek 2*. But as I was about to get up during the credits, Hintsa ran back. 'Mommy, can YOU take me to the bathroom?'

I looked at him in the lightening theatre. 'Hey Papi. But I thought you were going with your father?'

'He stopped to talk to some lady outside and he's still talking to her. Please hurry mommy, it's urgent.' I grabbed my bag and hurried out, planning to give Mandla a piece of my mind about flirting in the lobby when I was done taking the boy to the bathroom. But I had nothing to be worried about. The woman Mandla was talking to was fatter than me, and not the best-looking chick on the block. I hurried a 'Hello' as I rushed Hintsa to the bathroom. Must be some Sowetan nurse from Bara who knew Mandla from his stint there. On my return, she was gone.

We had our dinner like the perfect family that we are, and made tracks to Siz and Vuyo's home so Mandla and I could have a night out and be the perfect couple that we are.

Upon our arrival, Pertunia took Hintsa off our hands, gave him a bath and tucked him in with the two younger Vuyos. She was really good. Even Vuyo senior, who had initially called her 'a "Jim comes to Joburg" rural chick who could add no value to the household' was starting to show begrudging appreciation for her. I could see his eyes light up as she talked to his children – he probably noticed she paid them more attention than his wife did.

As usual, Vuyo and Siz, in their designer wear, made us look like rural relatives. Vuyo was wearing a Hugo Boss suit, with cufflinks that you know he could not afford on his wages. If clothes maketh the man, then Vuyo was definitely The Man! Siz looked like the perfect partner in her brown and orange Chanel just-above-the-knee dress, a cute little orange clutch from the same designer house, and a pair of sling-back shoes that I would sell my husband for. Mandla and I, in *my* mind the perfect couple, now just looked like a dowdy pair in our 'special' Woollies threads. Mandla, perhaps sensing my dwindling confidence, grabbed my ass as we walked into the club and whispered, 'I don't care what anyone says, I still think my wife has the best-looking ass in Joburg.' I knew what he was trying to do. I arched my eyebrows and asked, 'Only in Joburg?' Boy, I loved this man.

After our night of debauchery, we were back at Siz's house around eleven the next morning with killer hangovers. I walked in yelling, 'VUUUYO! Man, where are you with a

Bloody Mary?' It was Pertunia who answered, 'He is still sleeping. Maybe you should leave him, but Nosizwe is up and I can tell her you are here.' Whew, talk of Eve giving orders! And I noticed that she had just referred to Siz by her name and not 'Auntie Nosizwe' like she had always done. But, noting that my son was clean and happy I just thanked Pertunia for looking after him. We must have looked like a couple of alcoholics, asking for a hangover cure so early in the day – maybe that's why Pertunia was a trifle abrupt with me, I thought. Maids are, after all, very protective.

Siz came into the reception room behind Pertunia, picking up a toy that one of the children had left on her ivory carpet. 'Sis Pertunia, have you cleaned the house today?' She sounded just like her mother as we followed her into the living room, and her loud voice was playing havoc with my hangover. 'And look at this. When was the last time you dusted this TV stand? Honestly, I do not know what I pay you for sometimes.'

To which Pertunia responded, in one of those typical sulky-maid voices that sound as though they are talking to themselves but in effect want you to hear, '*Uyandisokolisa uNosizwe*. I can't do everything at once. I had to wash the children and feed them, and cook and clean. I have a schedule for when I do the dusting in the house but some people, who cannot even cook, want you to do everything.'

Siz, naturally, heard and as she opened her mouth I went and closed it with my hand because I could see that, between Siz's hangover temperament and the maid who wasn't amused at her work being questioned, I could end up not getting any tomato juice for my Bloody Mary. So I kissed her, gave her a pat on her annoyingly perfect backside and said, '*Hawu, Sis Pertunia. Uyazi kuthi uSiz uyadlala nawe.* This house looks very clean for a place with two children. Eish, my house doesn't even look this neat and I have only one child so not to worry, *ibabalasi kuphela*. But now for my hangover cure *s'thando sami*, since you are the woman of this house, I know where the bar is but where is the tomato juice?'

And she answered, '*Ja ndiyazi* but there are people who don't appreciate all the work,' and Siz, wanting to save herself from an angry maid said, '*Ndiyaxolisa* Sis Pertunia. Thandi is right, I overreacted.' And with a mischievous grin she added, '*S'right s'thando*?' which Pertunia ignored. She placed two cans of tomato juice in my hands and said, 'I will take the bus to my class today.'

Siz and I shared a look, and Mandla said, 'Damn Siz, you got one pissed off maid.' To which Siz responded, 'Who is saving me on petrol with her outburst. I think I'll ask Vuyo to pick her up from her classes. Because if I go, she might ignore me. And that way I can take a nap.' As she spoke, Mandla got a funny look on his face. 'Talking of that man of yours, where is he? By this time all the Sowetan drinkers are on their fifth drink. He seems to be forgetting his roots now he's in suburbia.'

When Mandla left the room to go and wake Vuyo up, Siz continued worrying about Pertunia. 'Pertunia's been like this for the last few days. I don't know what her problem is. Eish, sometimes maids can be problematic.'

'Maybe she is PMSing,' I offered. 'Or maybe she misses her children in the Eastern Cape. When are you giving her leave?'

Siz answered, 'Girl, she better forget about leave until Vuyo's kids go on school holidays. Who would cook for all the Vuyos? You know I can't cook to save my ass.'

'You must cherish Pertunia, man,' I told her. 'Ay, I hope to high heavens that I will be so blessed, and Marita is as good a worker as Pertunia.'

Siz started laughing, 'I think now you are smoking some bad shit because you know your white maid will be whining about blisters just from using the feather duster on those two-hundred and one Biko and Sobukwe framed posters of yours.'

As I was telling her to shut it, the men walked in. After our Bloody Marys, and after hearing Hintsa ask for the umpteenth time when we were going to pick up Marita, we left. On our way out, Siz suggested, 'Hey Mister and Missis, why don't we get together for drinks with Lauren and Mike later on this evening? I haven't spoken to that girl all week.'

I told her it was a good idea, 'But maybe tomorrow. Better if Marita just unpacks today before we throw her to Lauren.'

Marita was blown away when we showed her the cottage. Her eyes lit up, she laughed a deep guttural laugh and said, '*Jissus*, this is mine? I never had my own television before!' This sent her on a reminiscing trip, 'You know when I was growing up we had this small black and white TV, the picture was so unclear. And when I got married, the bastard man always wanted to hold the remote control. He wouldn't let me watch anything if I didn't make him enough money!' I was glad she liked her cottage, but her enthusiasm seemed a little OTT to me. I was never really good with people thanking me, anyway. It was embarrassing. So I just said, 'Make yourself at home, tomorrow I will show you around.' One might suppose that she was receiving too much privilege for a maid, but I partly did it for selfish, snobbish reasons – so that I could still maintain my space with my family and not fraternise with the help. This was, naturally, very different from Lauren's outlook, but that is because Lauren enjoys having a constantly full house. I often wonder why she doesn't seem to miss having time to herself with just her husband and kids.

I was looking forward to the working week ahead as I have one of those gratifying civil service jobs where you get to be your own boss. As Executive Director of a Soweto office for the provincial Department of Tourism, I find my job highly satisfying – I daresay had I not met Mandla before I started the job I would still be single, fully satisfied, working late each day and creating new goals for myself.

My immediate superior is the Director General of Tourism in the Minister's Office, a useless chap who is one of those remnants from the apartheid era who seems to be our token white guy – another interesting aspect of this country we all love. I've noticed that in the 'New South Africa', to use an overused and abused term, corporations usually employ a token black person to show that they are willing to transform, and government usually keeps a token white person to prove that the blacks are not taking over everything in the country and giving all the jobs to their relatives. This is how we in the DOT got saddled with our boss. JD (Johann du Preez, not to be confused with the hip-hop JD) as we all call him, seems to have zero knowledge of tourism. He had no idea where the Hector Peterson Museum was, or even *who* Hector Peterson was, last time he was here and I had the pleasure of taking him on a tour of places of interest in Johannesburg. And he seems content in his ignorance, unless he feels someone wants his job. Fortunately for him, none of us provincial EDs want his job, because we are glad to have our own fiefdoms far away from Pretoria, sorry *Tshwane*, politics. All of us, however, have to write him monthly reports on what we are up to, and his poor PA has to compile these into one document every time JD has to pretend to the head honcho (Mr Minister) that he is actually working and overseeing all provinces satisfactorily. It's a small price to pay to stay away from Tshwane: a town mired in apartheid traditions even to this day – I visit there only if I absolutely have to.

The beauty of having offices in Soweto is that, nowadays, it seems to be the 'in' place for tourists coming to Gauteng. The other beauty of working in Soweto is that when I am not involved with my usual hectic schedule (read: when I do not create a busy schedule for myself), I get to drive to and from work with Mandla, since he has set up his surgery in Soweto.

Mandla, by the way, is a cardiologist who initially got into medicine because he 'wanted to make a difference'. After six months working at Bara upon his return from Harvard Med, he realised that making a difference may make your conscience feel great but it seldom pays the bills.

So he set up shop – a surgery and pharmacy – with two friends in Orlando West.

His colleagues are Chukwu Anyaokwu, a Nigerian divorcé, Romeo, and surgeon (in that order), and the pharmacist, Kamau Kariithi. The three of them do a pretty splendid business: Chukwu charms, Mandla listens, and Kamau has a marvellous Kikuyu thrift that keeps the business side going. Their patients love them. Apparently though, the doctors deal more with sexually transmitted infections and dispensing Anti-Retroviral Treatments than anything they specialised in.

Mandla having a surgery works out well for both of us as it ensures one of us has a normal nine to five schedule, and this is the reason he is the listed emergency contact at Hintsa's pre-school.

I love Mondays, I really do, because they hold the promise of a fresh start. However, this was not the case today. On arrival at the office my useless deputy had bungled the budget I am supposed to submit to the DG by tomorrow for our annual financial report. I was stuck with doing all the facts and figures, in addition to rushing to Ubuntu Kraal at lunchtime to ensure that the logistics for the four-day conference starting the next day would run smoothly and guarantee us more American conferences in future. At the end of the day, I carried my work home on a laptop so I could complete and email the budget before I went to bed.

As if that were not bad enough, my bloody maid showed that she is total trailer trash and unused to cleaning floor tiles. Despite my having Cobra One-Step in the cleaning cabinet, she had mopped the floors with water and soap, leaving streaks all over. To add salt to the wound, she took it upon herself to be 'helpful' by making supper. The supper comprised boiled ribs (who the hell boils ribs?) swimming in water and oil, with tomatoes, onions and green pepper for company. The starch component was half-cooked rice. Did this woman think my family was gonna eat this? I take my food very seriously (my bum did not get this big from nothing). I get extra-annoyed when a meal is badly prepared, which accounts for why I don't often eat at other people's houses.

I knew she meant well but, having already had a sucky day, I could not find it in me to be diplomatic and went to bang on her door. She opened the door still wearing the pink two-piece work uniform that I had bought her. I started on a polite note, asking her how her day was. 'Oh, very nice,' she gushed. 'I met MaRosie next door and she said she will take me to see Pertunia and we can go for tea over there.'

Ja ja ja. I didn't want a blow-by-blow account of her day, I just wanted her not to mess up my house. So I thanked her for making dinner, told her that was not one of her duties since Mandla and I preferred to cook for ourselves, and that anyway I had brought Chinese home. 'I have left the food for you, why don't you come by and get it so you won't need to cook tomorrow?' I added, thinking to myself that my maid almost made Siz seem like a good cook. Almost, but not quite. Why couldn't she be more like Pertunia, who was as gourmet a chef as a maid can ever be?

When she came into the house to get her boiled ribs and half-cooked rice, I gave her blow-by-blow instructions on how to mop the floor. Can you believe having to teach a thirty-five-year-old woman such a fundamental? Damn, and I thought madamhood was going to be easy. Men never seem to straighten maids out in any home situation, and this always makes madams look like queen bitches. It makes me wonder, are maids a male conspiracy to destroy female camaraderie?

CHAPTER 6

The Confrontation

I was trying to adjust to madamhood, but there were still a few kinks to be sorted. Sure, the house was spotless. But she had messed up my walk-in closet with her colour-coded tidying; my orderly mess was nowhere to be seen and I could not find my favourite jeans because, with her colour system, I would have to hunt them down among my blue suits. Mandla had adjusted better than me, although she had put a crease in his jeans. With his characteristic good humour he had just smiled, called her over and demonstrated on the ironing board how he liked his jeans ironed.

Even the first meeting between my white maid and Lauren was an anticlimax. On Thursday, I took Marita over to introduce her, bearing a gift of shepherd's pie for the psuedo-Brits. Lauren had a jaw-on-the-floor moment, but quickly collected herself. Maybe all that careful studying of royal decorum and rules of protocol had actually paid off?

By Friday morning, I was seriously considering whether having a maid was worth it. I had made my point to Lauren. Now I was thinking that maybe it was time to let go of the experiment. I was considering finding somewhere else for her to go when I got to the office and realised that I had left my laptop at home.

Making my way home again to pick up my laptop, I kept weighing up different options. Marita was really good with Hintsa, but she was also really intruding in my personal space. Hintsa was five, I had done without a maid since he was born, although, I had to admit, not without some stress to myself.

It turns out Marita's relocation from my house wasn't to be. She must not have heard my car in the driveway because as I walked in, one of my James Brown albums was blasting from the stereo and Marita was holding the mop like a mike, dancing as only a white girl who's been around black people in prison can, and singing loudly: 'Say it LOUD: I am BLACK and I am PROUD!'

You are WHAT? It was such a comic moment I could not control my laughter. When she heard me, she whirled around with a guilty look, 'Sorry Madam, I was just mopping the floor ...' She quickly switched off the stereo.

'Not to worry, I'm just here to pick up my laptop,' I answered, there and then deciding there was no way I could fire a white Afrikaans girl who sang 'I'm black and I'm proud'. Marita would stay. If only for comic relief.

As I was leaving I had a thought. 'Marita?'

'Yes madam?' she answered, head held low.

'No need to keep calling me madam, you are part of the family now, you can call me MaHintsa, like MaRosie and everyone else does.'

'Oh, thank you maaad ... I mean, MaHintsa,' she said.

I had been feeling a trifle guilty. The whole work week had been so busy that I had been an inattentive mother and wife, too tired to listen to Hintsa's school-day stories and too tired to make love to my husband. Fortunately for me, Mandla was an alright cook. Not as good as my dad, but good enough to make dinner for himself and the boy during the week. I know Mandla enjoys cooking, but I still feel guilty for not performing my 'womanly role'. It must be inborn or drummed into me by society that I am supposed to do the cooking and cleaning, in spite of claiming to be a feminist.

We managed to do our Friday night family outing, which made me feel a little less guilty. On Saturday Mandla woke up slapping his forehead.

'What have you forgotten now?' I asked.

'Oh babes. I am so sorry.'

'For what? Did you forget to take out the rubbish again?'

Looking sheepish he turned to me with what he thought was his irresistible, apologetic, puppy-dog look. 'Eish babes. I forgot to tell you that I invited my colleagues and their partners for dinner today. You don't have any plans, do you?'

Man. I thought he had failed to tell me that an asteroid was about to hit Earth. People over for dinner and a chance to show my culinary skills? I laughed, 'Have no fear. Thandi the Superwoman is here.' Then I wondered out loud whether I should call my father for suggestions as to what to make for the guests.

Mandla was not amused. 'Why do you always have to call your father regarding anything culinary? He is not here and I'm the one that will be eating the food. Why don't you make your stir-fry chicken strips and some pasta? I really like that.'

'Oooh. Why are you so touchy about daddy? You know he would give Jamie Oliver and Martha Stewart a run for their money in the kitchen. Or are you still pissed off that he thought your dinner was crap last time he was here?' I rubbed against him suggestively to make him focus his brain on something else. It wasn't difficult, and soon the bedroom door had been locked in case of a five-year-old's intrusion.

Having worked up an appetite in the bedroom, I snacked on a sandwich while I planned my dinner party. What to cook? I decided to go with my husband's suggestion and stir-fry chicken strips with vegetables and serve them with angel hair pasta, red pepper, fresh thyme and grated cheddar. Mandla would make the salad – he makes the best salad in the world, after famous Hawaiian restaurateur Sam Choy of the 'Never trust a skinny chef' T-shirts fame.

With my menu arranged, I proceeded to marinade my chicken in spices and a touch of white wine. My son walked in yawning and rubbing his eyes with his little fists. 'Hey there sweets. How is my favourite man in the whole wide world?' I bent down to kiss him. 'Did you sleep well?'

'Uhh. Mommy, I am going next door to Auntie Lauren's.' Well so much for mommy's favourite man wanting to be with his mother. Wasn't it just yesterday that he crawled behind me everywhere I went?

'Not in your PJ's you ain't. And make sure you brush your teeth first,' I said, walking him to the bathroom.

'I don't know why you always make me brush my teeth when I get up,' he complained. 'My teacher told me that we should brush our teeth after every meal. And since I brush my teeth before I go to bed, and when I wake up I haven't had any meal, why do you want me to do it?'

I told him to put his hand over his mouth and smell his breath.

'Eeeuw,' he said with a disgusted look on his face.

'See? At night the Evil Tooth Witch comes while you're sleeping and throws stinky magic dust in your mouth.'

I knew I would not have to persuade him to brush his teeth ever again. By the time he would know that there was no Evil Tooth Witch, he would be too busy trying to impress the opposite sex to be caught with sour morning breath.

With the child next door and out of my hair, and Mandla off to the surgery for a few hours, I called Siz. 'Just when are you coming over for our weekly brunch?'

'On my way, and I have two bottles of wine with your and Lauren's names written all over them. I had to go and drop Pertunia at her class. Gimme twenty minutes,' she said.

Although this was Marita's first week, it seemed she had fitted right into the community of maids. After the call to Siz, I wandered out to the Vibracrete wall that separated my house from Lauren's and saw Marita deep in conversation with MaRosie.

When they saw me, Marita furiously began beating her doormat against the wall and MaRosie pretended to clean the broom that she was holding.

"*Haibo*, are you talking about me to suddenly stop your conversation?' They both looked guilty. 'MaRosie, can you call MaJunior please?'

Lauren walked over to her side of the fence, 'And how may I be of assistance?' Darling Lauren, ever so formal. 'Girl, I am starving. You still remember that you are supposed to bring muffins to my place for brunch, right?'

'I've just finished baking them. I'll just check with Mike if it's okay for me to come over,' she answered.

'Girl you need to stop "checking with Mike" on everything. You are going next door, you ain't going to Mars. Tell him Junior can watch the kids. See you in fifteen minutes, alright?' I was a little annoyed at this characteristic of Lauren's, always asking Mike permission for everything.

I turned to Marita, as Lauren Lovelyface waddled back into her house. 'So what are you doing with your day off Ms Black and Proud?'

'I'm going shopping with MaRosie as soon as she has finished washing and dressing all the children, and then Pertunia will come and meet us after her class and we'll get lunch at Chicken Licken,' she answered, sounding proud of her networking abilities with the other maids.

I felt like a snobbish, petit bourgeois madam, but I was curious to know how a fifty-year-old overworked and underpaid black maid and a thirty-five-year old overpaid and underworked white maid had become gossip partners over the wall.

'Well, on Monday when I picked up Hintsa from school, as soon as he returned he went next door. I couldn't see where he was, but when I heard his voice I went over there to shout at him. MaRosie told me he almost always stays there because you and Junior's mother are friends. She said we should *maar* go for tea at Pertunia's house the next day and that's how I met Pertunia. She is very pretty, but MaRosie's very nice. I like her, I mean I like them both, but I like MaRosie more.'

Maids are an interesting species. They take ownership of anything that belongs to their madams. I had not missed the way Marita had referred to Siz's house as Pertunia's. Just like in the adverts, when the madams are away, the maids play. Naturally, Siz did not know about the tea. I guess Marita had not yet learnt that there are certain things one should keep from the madams!

Then she whispered confidentially in a deep Afrikaans accent which twelve years in a Jozi jail had done nothing to erase, 'You know Rosie?' to which I answered in the affirmative. 'She has been complaining about MaJunior hey? She said every morning she is the first to wake up and the last to go to bed and she says that I am so lucky.' I knew exactly why MaRosie thought Marita was lucky, but it's always nice to hear compliments about yourself so I asked, 'Why does she think you are lucky?'

'Well you see, because all I need to do is just clean the house, hang the washing to dry and do the ironing, and help Hintsa with his homework but her … Eish! She has to cook, clean, wash the dishes, hand wash most of the laundry even though there is a washing machine, and cook all the meals since morning. I told her she must call the Union because you are very kind and MaJunior is not.'

COSATU caused us problems. Even people without specialised experience in anything were talking about unions. God. It was good that Marita was talking to MaRosie though. So long as the only competition I had as an employer was Lauren, I was sure to always emerge smelling of roses to my maid.

The girls walked in at the same time – Siz had left her step kids with the other children next door – just as Mandla was walking out.

'Hey both of yous,' I welcomed them. 'What do y'all have with you?'

'Brought some cheese muffins baked this morning don't you know?' Lauren answered with a click of the fingers and a wave of the head à la Ricki Lake, to titters from Siz and I. Good attempt, but she still sounded like an uppercrust Brit.

I took the muffins, which smelled fantastic, and turned to Siz. 'You need to let Lauren and I give you a tutorial in cooking. I have no idea how you can be sooo lacking in culinary skills, since Ma is such a fab cook.' Mandla and I had been talking about Siz's Ma just the other day, and how in our own weird, probably masochistic way, we miss her. (She is always dragging us over the coals whenever she is around.) 'How is Ma, anyway?'

'Girl,' Siz rolled her eyes and looked petulant. 'I don't know how she is. Better ask her first-born Lauren, or call her favourite child Lizwe. You know I don't even call her because I get tired of hearing how I married the wrong man and how I can't do anything right. I only call her if I have to relay a message, and I always make sure I am rushing off somewhere so I don't have to talk to her for long.'

Lauren chimed, 'I do not know why you don't appreciate your mother, Siz. She is the classiest person I have ever known. You two could learn something from her, judging by your speech. But since you ask, Thandi, Ma thinks she has a bit of 'flu, but otherwise she's well. She just sent me some press clippings of Prince William and his latest girl-friend from the *Daily Mail*. She thinks the girl is not as pretty as my Elizabeth, but since we are saving Lizzie for spirited Prince Harry, I really don't mind.'

Siz and I looked at each other and almost barfed. What was it with Ma and Lauren and their Royal Obsession? Ma had been torturing me with newspaper cuttings since I was in university, and I'm sure Siz has been getting them all her life. When I get her cuttings, with her little red ink 'editorial' captions, I just dump them in the bin. Figuring if we let Lauren go on we would never be able to discuss anything else, I put a stop to it. 'MaJunior, we are here to brunch and drink, so if you tell us about your and Ma's 'tea with the queen' plans one more time I think Siz and I will have to throw you out.'

Lauren wasn't having it, 'The problem with the two of you is that you are not cultured enough to appreciate the monarch. Fortunately I am capable, to paraphrase Kipling, of drinking with commoners and not losing my virtue. And I can walk with kings – or the royal family – without losing the common touch.'

To which Siz answered sarcastically, 'Yeah. I can see how not appreciating an old lady who wears flowery dresses, has a husband who believes there are UFOs, a first son who dabbles in alternative medicine and a grandson who smokes more *zol* than Mandla and Vuyo put together is not being cultured. And who are you calling common, Ms *plaasmeisie*?'

This was fast getting out of hand, someone had to put a stop to their sticks and stones. 'Whatever, you two, can we get on with the business of brunching and drinking please,' this from a Thandi practising for when she finally got the role of Edwina in *Absolutely Fabulous*. Not to mention that I needed to be tipsy to appreciate the run-in that I knew Siz and Lauren were going to have regarding Marita at some point in time.

'Hey Thandi, your house looks really clean. I have never seen it this tidy before. No marks on your kitchen table, no dust on the TV stand, no finger marks on your beige walls, and I like the way the couches have been moved. Makes it really spacious, and look at where you have that Biko portrait now, looks good,' commented Lauren as I whipped up some omelettes. I wasn't ready to go into the merits and demerits of my maid, what with all the redecorating she had done (without seeking my input), so I just diverted her by asking whether I should cook something up for the children. 'Oh no, MaRosie made them a huge pancake breakfast before she left,' she answered.

Siz poured the champagne, looked sombre, and raised her glass.

'Ladies, let's be serious a moment. I want to propose a toast.' I had a feeling she was about to say some crazy thing, as was her habit.

Instead she said, 'Lauren, here is to you girl. Thanks for

training your man so well that he is out there looking after the brood while we are in here about to get smashed.' Lauren and I tittered as we all toasted and downed.

She responded, 'As both of you know, Michael and I have been together since university. Well, to respond to your toast, I have told you both that men are like dogs. I got mine when he was a puppy so he is well trained.' Now we were straight out laughing – until she added in a stage whisper, 'although sometimes he bites.' Had we heard her right? I shrugged my shoulders; Siz raised her eyebrows. Lauren and her peculiarities.

More champagne was poured and, as was traditional in our circle, the victim would become the victrix of witticism. Lauren raised her glass to me. 'And here's to the doctor's wife. For the husband who knows when he is not wanted …' more laughter, then Lauren continued less loudly, 'and for joining the club of Madams.' We toasted and downed, but this time around the champagne tasted that bit less sweet. We all knew there were underlying issues behind the Madam statement. Could it be that the girl was still displeased about her black neighbour hiring a white maid, even though she had had almost a week to get used to it?

It was up to me to restore the humour with my toast, so I poured more champagne, winked at Siz and said, 'And here's to my old friend, Siz. I wish I could find something better to toast you for than, "to your Mandingo man!"'

The lightheartedness was back. This was fun, in spite of Lauren being a little quieter than usual. For one crazy afternoon we could pretend it was a woman's world and men just live in it.

Brunch was good. We polished off the two bottles of champagne and I brought out a bottle of white wine, which we consumed while Siz washed the dishes, I dried and

Lauren cleared the table – and then the shit hit the fan.

It was started by Lauren, who, it can be assumed, needed the waters of Dionysius to loosen her tongue. 'So what is going on, Thandi?' Lauren threw the question at me sounding just as I had always assumed sixteenth century inquisitors would sound. I knew well what she was talking about, but I wanted her to spell it out, so I looked at her questioningly.

'Why must you plead ignorance when you know exactly what I mean? Why didn't you tell me you were getting someone to assist you in the house when you let everyone else know? I thought we were friends.'

Excuse you?

'Sorry hon, I didn't know I had to consult you on every minute change in my life, including the fact that I am getting domestic help. And why should I tell you anyway? Is my maid's salary coming out of your esteemed lecturer pockets?'

'When you came over with Marita you told me that she came from the halfway house. You took Siz with you. So I'm just asking why Siz knew and I didn't. I thought we were all friends.' She was milking the hurt.

Thixo. Now bloody Lauren was gonna put up the 'equally good friend' smokescreen to try to cover her initial shock at finding that I had employed a white woman as my maid. Her next statement really cleared any doubt my befuddled and half-drunk mind might have had.

'I mean,' she continued, 'if you had told me you were serious about needing a maid, I could have asked Rosie to ask her sister …'

Big mistake. It seemed she had just stoked Nosizwe's fire. 'Enlighten me, Lauren,' Siz jumped in. 'Is the fuckin' problem the fact that you wanted to help Rosie's sister, the fact that Thandi has a maid and didn't tell you about it, or is it that she has a WHITE MAID and this offends your sense of decorum and your idea of the order of things?'

The best thing about white people is that they wear their emotions on their skin. Tensing as if she had been slapped and getting all red in the face, Lauren cursed in her best offended-English-ma'am tone, 'I am not talking to you, you bloody cow!' She was looking at Sizwe, managing to sound offended while still being proper and not raising her voice. But she was fluttering her hands, clearly agitated. 'You always have to bring race into it. I do not care whatever race someone's maid is, but if Thandi had told me there was a lady who needed help at the halfway house I would have tried to get her a job as a telephonist at Wits or something.'

Contradiction? Yes it was, and Siz pounced on it. 'Hooked her up as a telephonist? Why don't you go ahead and do that for Rosie's sister? Is she too black to be a 'lady' and answer the telephone?'

'How dare you?' Lauren shrieked, the proper lady getting lost somewhere as she threw the full contents of her wine glass in Siz's face.

We had all definitely drunk a little too much, but somehow I never thought this was going to get physical. Siz slapped Lauren and I tried to step in the middle to calm both of them, but they were too far gone, and all I got was both of them yelling at me, 'Stay out of this Thandi. This is between the two of us.'

Okay, that would have made a lot of sense had they not been in my house, fighting about my maid. I was tempted to club both of them with a rolling pin. As I pulled it from my kitchen drawer, Lauren somehow managed to trip Siz to the ground and sit on her (with all of her 89 kgs). Siz, for her part, was not giving up and grabbed a fistful of Lauren's curly blonde tresses. It was then that my son walked in, dripping wet.

'Aunt Lo! Aunt Siz! I wanna play too!' That got their attention. Lauren heaved herself up awkwardly trying, to no avail, for some semblance of dignity, with Siz following after. 'I was just showing Aunt Siz a wrestling manoeuvre but we're all done now,' she told him.

Siz, never to be outdone, stuttered, 'And I was just showing Aunt Lo that getting your hair pulled really hurts.' At which point I attempted to distract with mock anger, 'Boy. What are you doing dripping on my floor?'

He had apparently forgotten to get a beach towel. I got it for him from the bathroom and told him to go and fetch the little Vuyos as Aunt Siz was 'just leaving'. I looked pointedly at both of them. I wasn't having these drunken fools in my house a minute longer to break my furniture. Lauren followed Hintsa outside with Siz behind her, both of them glaring at me as if I was the one who had wronged them.

CHAPTER 7

Friendless

Saturday night, with Mandla's colleagues Chukwu and Kamau and their partners, was entertaining and took my mind off the sudden exit of Siz and Lauren. Charming Chukwu, who brought his groupie-of-the-moment, Lerato, reverted to his sexist self after a few drinks.

'Your wife really knows how to feed a man, Mandla. She was worth all the cattle you paid for her I am sure. Though it may not be such a good idea to keep her working. She probably had you changing diapers when Hintsa was a child.'

I was not in the mood for his baiting and just ignored him but Kamau's wife, Njeri, a diminutive dark beauty with a feminist passion that belied her size, staunchly defended. 'I would ignore that stupid statement Chukwu, but I cannot believe that the South African government with its great Constitution gave you a permit to stay and practise in South Africa. What kind of hole did you creep out of in Nigeria, where all women do is cook and clean?'

Rise to the bait and you are sure to get more thrown at you. Now Kamau chimed in, 'But sweetie, you must admit the Bible had it right when it said, "Man is the head of the House".'

Njeri turned on her husband, 'Which verse and chapter? I hate it when you MCPs revert to quoting the Bible when it suits you. I hope the house that you head is not the same one that I am paying mortgage on, because that is the most idiotic thing I have ever heard from you in all our eight years of marriage.' And seeing my silence and hoping to bring another woman on board, Njeri turned to Lerato. 'Don't you think these men are ridiculous, Lerato?'

Lerato, knowing where her bread was buttered (or to be more precise, who paid for her Hunter's Dry) mumbled, 'Umm, well. I think Chukwu is right.' Njeri couldn't believe it. 'Oh–ho. You think Chukwu is right? Exactly what do you do for a living, Lerato?' Oh boy, it was getting hot in here.

Mandla rushed in to play excellent host. 'Don't worry about it Njeri. For what it's worth, I think,' winking at Chukwu, 'that Chukwu is a sexist pig and there was absolutely nothing wrong with my changing my son's diapers. And Chukwu, even you know that we wouldn't be here without strong women supporting us all the way. I know I would not be what I am without the support of my mother and sisters, and now, my wife.'

'Aw. Kamau,' Njeri said, punching him lightly on the arm, 'Why can't you learn to be more like Mandla? You would definitely be getting more sex if you did.'

'I thought you said you liked a man's man?' Kamau shot back. 'You have to admit Mandla is a bit of a metrosexual, with all that nappy-changing stuff.'

'Yeah, but it is kind of sexy. Frankly I think Beckham is more of a babe than Idi Amin ever was, even at his richest and most powerful moment,' she answered back, always anxious to have the last word.

And then I jumped in, 'I hate to be on Chukwu's side regarding this one, but metrosexual men are really not that sexy Njez. Imagine battling in front of the mirror with your man to see who looks better? Besides, if the good Lord wanted Adam to go to the spa, he would not have created girlfriends!'

Speaking of which, it seemed I now had none. The morning after 'The Great Catfight', as it had been dubbed by the men in our lives, I saw Lauren over the wall and greeted her. Homegirl looked right through me as if I weren't there. And when I called Siz, I overheard her telling Pertunia, who answered the phone, 'If it's Lauren tell her to hold on and if it's Thandi tell her I am not here.' Hold up. This girl just had a fight in my house with Lauren and yet she would rather talk to Lauren than me? You would think that I had instigated their catfight.

Okay. Maybe I had, indirectly, by hiring Marita. But should I have to justify my maid to any of them? Besides, Siz thought it was a brilliant idea at the time and Marita was doing a good job with my son. Bloody heifers. I have my man, my son and my job and if they are going to be juvenile about everything then they have probably been a waste of my time anyway... so long suckers!

When I told Mandla how my Former Friends had treated me, he mouthed some regrets about the whole situation and told me I should talk to them in about two weeks when we'd all calmed down. I would be damned if I was going to make the first step to the negotiating table.

'They can damn well come to me. I am not the one who told them they should start fighting. In fact babes, I tried to stop them fighting,' I said.

And Mandla answered not too wisely, 'Yeah babe, but you threw them out of your house.'

'Excuse you? Whose side are you on anyway? I am supposed to be your wife. So you think it's all my fault? Fine.

But tell me, would you have allowed people to fight and cause a mess when you are expecting guests? I have an ivory carpet for crying out loud!' I added, mumbling, 'Not that it means anything to you. I am supposed to deal with all the issues, you just expect a clean house and a witty wife to impress your friends with.'

Mandla sensed that he had handled it badly. 'Of course not babes.'

'Of course not, what? You don't expect a witty wife or I am not witty?'

Knowing that he was treading on eggshells, Mandla quickly manoeuvred. 'Of course not, it wasn't your fault and I don't expect you to let people fight in the house when we are expecting guests and mess up everything. I think I would have done the same thing, and have I told you your bum looks fabulous in those jeans?'

'Really?' I said, analysing myself in one of the full-length mirrors I had placed in the entrance corridor to 'give it space', as per Oprah's advice. 'Yeah it does, doesn't it? I thought I was putting on a little weight, though.'

'Putting on weight? You? Never. You look as good as before Hintsa was born,' said my man, coming closer. He could have meant two months before our son was born, but I wasn't going to analyse it. Mandla was the only person on my side and for now, I would cherish the moment.

But he too betrayed me the very next day by inviting Vuyo and Mike over for drinks. Mike, a little too lasciviously, I thought, started with, 'So how was the fight? Who was on top?' The dude was probably having some fantasy of the two women oiled and wrestling each other for his affections. Oh, to be a simple man. They seem to want so little from life except cars, sex and beer. I couldn't be wasting my time detailing their sexual fantasies, so I went to take a nap.

I was beginning to realise how cold it was on my own, though, and with Mandla at the surgery even during the weekend, I could not stand it. Until the fight, I had not appreciated how much I relied on my open door policy with Lauren. Here I had been thinking that she was just the white girl next door, and now I realised what an important person she had become in my life.

The worst thing was, I had no idea why my girlfriends were freezing me out. What the hell? I started to send Marita over to pick up my son from next door each day. 'Mommy, are you not friends with Auntie Lauren anymore?' he asked eventually.

I could not lie. 'Darling, mommy and Aunt Lauren just had a bit of an argument, but we will talk about it when we are both ready.'

'So is it okay for me to still go to Auntie Lauren's house and play with Diana?' he asked, perhaps feeling as though he was betraying his mother. Guilt ate at me. Was I in danger of destroying my son's social life because of my pride? But they are the ones who had ignored me! *They* were destroying *my* social life. Shit.

The truth was, I missed gossiping over the wall to Lauren about the kids. I missed getting my daily horoscope from her. I missed hearing the latest babymama drama from Siz. I missed moaning about Mandla to sympathetic ears.

Two weeks into the Thandi freeze-out, I came back from work to see Siz's car parked outside Lauren's house. Siz, who was so obsessed with her work she never visited anyone during the week. Maybe they were both trying to make a point. And when I peeped outside at nine in the evening, her car was still there. Cows!

As if their absence in my life was not tough enough, my maid was gossiping with MaRosie and would lie low and pretend to be cleaning every time she saw me coming. Having been Miss Popularity all my life, I was beginning to understand how all those fat girls with zits who we used to tease must have felt. This pariah lifestyle was not for me. I called my daddy to complain (and also in the hope that he would relay the message to Vuyo, who could talk to his wife). 'What's going on?' he asked.

'Daddy. Two weeks ago, Lauren and Siz had a fight in my house and I kicked them out. I called them the next day but they both refused to talk to me and they are still freezing me out.'

'Oh, the famous fight?'

'Daddy, how did you know about the fight?' I asked, not a little surprised.

'Vuyo told me when I talked to him the other day. Baby you should try to patch things up, because you girls need each other. All may not be as it seems.'

'What are you talking about, daddy?' I felt panicked.

'Just what I am telling you. Try to talk to Vuyo and Mike and find out what's upsetting the girls and why they refuse to talk to you. Bite the bullet and make up with your friends, you stubborn girl,' he said sternly.

'Daddy, you know me better than that. They can damn well come to me. I called Siz the other day and she wouldn't take my call, and Lauren acts like I don't exist and I am right next door.'

'Well fine, do what you want,' my daddy sounded annoyed. 'But let me talk to my little man if he is there.'

'He is not here, he went to Lauren's house. I don't know why he can't just stay here and spend time with his mother,' I said feeling sorry for myself.

'Maybe his mother is a little too childish for him to stay around? Look Thandi, growing up is about forgiving each other. I have to go now. My farm assistant is here and he wants me to take him to Queenstown. I love you.'

'Yeah yeah, love you too daddy. But please talk to Vuyo for me and find out why they are so angry with me ...'

'Thandile, I told you I am not getting involved in the affairs of a grown woman. You miss your friends? You talk to their husbands and find out what's wrong.' And he hung up. My own father taking their side, and I do not even know what I did to them!

Why was everyone making it seem as though this whole fight was my fault? Even my maid was selling out – I overheard her telling MaRosie about how stubborn I was being. When she saw me, she knelt down and acted as if she was pulling out some weeds. As though I have stupid written on my forehead! Was I acting childish like my father accused me of being? If I had to answer honestly I would have to say yes. But then, the best bitch wars always are.

While I waited for my friends to realise the error of their ways, Marita and I became quite close, since I had no one else around to gossip with. I had got over being 'madam' and I was now just a simple MaHintsa and she, to Hintsa, was Auntie Marita.

'Off to the movies?' I asked one Saturday afternoon while lying in my hammock in the garden about to doze off. The boys had gone to visit granny in Soweto. I would miss Marita's presence on her day off because I no longer had friends.

'Ja,' she muttered, but I could see she had something confidential to impart, because she had that 'girlfriend gossip' look. I hoped it would be something that would get the girls and me talking again. When she said it though, I wished she had kept her mouth shut.

'*Hawu* MaHintsa, you won't believe what I heard!'

I smiled. Listening to her speak one could clearly tell that she had been spending way too much time with Ma-Rosie and Pertunia. I whispered back, imitating her conspiratorial tone.

'*Hawu* Aunt Marita, what did you hear?'

She laughed at my imitation, and then became serious. 'Yesterday we went to have tea with Pertunia. She showed us a necklace that she got from her boyfriend.'

So Pertunia had a boyfriend? Good. Maybe she would stop being so uptight. 'That's nice,' I responded indifferently. This was not worth taking up my Me-Time.

But Marita was persistent. 'Ja ... but you'll never guess who she said her boyfriend is?'

I cleaned an imaginary speck from my sunglasses and yawned. 'No. Who?'

'Vuyo,' she stated, knowing that I would immediately come to life.

'What?' I gasped, getting out of the hammock so fast I almost fell. 'Stop playing around like that Marita, that's not funny!' I yelled, gathering my dignity along with the spilled contents of the hammock.

'*Sirriaas,*' she said gravely.

Taking her hand, I led her to the table under the jacaranda tree, sat her down and made her tell me everything she knew.

'Well, I am not supposed to tell anyone really. Maybe this was a mistake. She said it was a secret for me and Ma-Rosie,' said Marita, a little hesitant.

'I said tell me everything you know Marita. Or you can damn well keep your secrets at Pertunia's house – oh that's right, she doesn't have one.'

Marita had never seen me like this. The madam had spoken so she answered.

'One day, about two months ago, Vuyo went home around lunch because he had forgotten something.' Marita leaned in towards me, looking around to make sure nobody was in earshot. 'He found Pertunia wrapped in a towel in their bedroom … putting on Siz's fancy make-up. She got one hell of a *skrik,* but what could she do?' Marita was really getting into her stride now – and I, of course, was a captive audience.

She leaned in closer. 'He asked what she was doing and she just looked at him like this,' Marita tipped her chin down and sucked in her cheeks, batting her eyelids in a disturbingly accurate impersonation of Pertunia the *Femme Fatale.* 'And she said: "What does it look like?" and then he said: "Well, you should do it more often" and then …' Marita dropped her voice to a hiss for the final revelation, '… he starts Brushing Her Hair!'

It seems one thing led to another and the rest, as they say, is history. Since that day, Vuyo the Rat had been going home to have his dalliance with his maid every lunch time, while his wife worked her perfectly toned butt off to keep a roof over his useless head. Talk about biting the hand that feeds you! It looked like Siz's mother had been right after all. Having dropped that bombshell, Marita happily went off to the movies, leaving me in mental turmoil. What to do?

Oh dammit. Why Siz? After all she had done for that fool and his horrible children. I needed a bloody drink. I walked up to the bar on the veranda and banged my fists on the bar counter, wishing it had been anything else, any-one else. Why Siz? Why would Vuyo do something like this to a woman who tried to give him everything? Ingrate!

I had no one to talk to about this except Mandla.

'Did you know that Vuyo was sleeping with Pertunia?' I demanded later that evening while Hintsa was having a bath and out of hearing.

Mandla responded in the affirmative, apparently more shocked at the fact that I had found out than about the indiscretions of Vuyo the Rat. He totally acted as if everything was normal … I could not understand it. In hindsight, of course, I should have known.

'*Uyazini*? I cannot believe you, Mandla. You don't want to know what I think of you right now for keeping something like this from me and Nosizwe! What else are you keeping from me?'

'Nothing man, babes. You are overreacting. I just did not think it was our business to be all up in their business.'

'*Hawu* Mandla! None of our business? What other family do we have on this side of Gauteng apart from Siz, Vuyo, Lauren and Mike?' Then it occurred to me that it might be a male conspiracy. I recalled the conversation I had had with my father. 'Do my father and Mike know?'

His slow nod made me regret all the times that I have ever broken a woman's confidence and told a man something. So this brotherhood thing was *deep*, even for men who had only become friends by virtue of their daughters and wives. BASTARDS!

'Tell you what *Bhuti?*' Now Mandla knew he was in for it. I never called him *Bhuti*, except when I was madder than a box of hungry scorpions.

'*Yini manje*?' he responded meekly.

'I know this is half your property so I am going to make it easy on both of us. Don't EVER bring Vuyo the Rat here when I am around and don't you dare tell him that I know what a rat he is. Or else you will be sleeping on the couch for the rest of your natural life. Got it?'

'What are you going to do?' Mandla looked defiant, in spite of his tongue-lashing. 'You suddenly going to start talking to Siz now? Will you call her and say, "Oh, so sorry about our fight, but I am calling to tell you your man has been dipping into your maid's cooking pot?"'

He had a point, but I was not going to let him win this one. I did not know what I was going to do, but after my threat of bedroom sanctions, I knew we had a deal.

Technically it *was* none of my business, as Mandla had already stated. But hell, Siz is my sister. We have been through thick and thin together. I also knew that, should the same thing ever happen to me, Siz would tell me. That's what sisterhood is all about, no? We had been through too much to keep something of this import from each other.

This had gone on long enough. Given what was at stake, I had to make the first move. Daddy was right, as usual. Besides, although Siz, Lauren and I had fought before, this was the longest we had gone without talking to each other.

I had to resolve this. I needed to resolve it not only because I missed my girls but, more importantly, so that I could find a way to break the news of Vuyo's infidelity to Siz. If she chose to stay with him, it would be her decision, but at least my conscience would not have to bear the burden. And, truth be told, I needed to resolve this so that I could 'be the bigger person' amongst us.

I am no Nobel Literature laureate, but have always been better at stating my emotions on paper. So I wrote them both a letter. I was of the opinion that this letter, if they read it and chose to feel me, would either result in us never talking to each other again, or have us re-examining our relationship and, hopefully, becoming better friends. I got on with it before I got cold feet. This is what it said:

Dear Madams (we all have maids and personal assistants so that is what we all are)
It has been almost a month since our fallout, the longest

time we have gone without talking to each other. I am writing this because I miss you guys. I am writing this because I am hoping we can mend the fences, but more importantly, because we all need to examine the dynamics of our friendship. In this, I will try to be as objective as possible, sparing no one, including myself. If either (or both) of you at this point do not feel we have anything worth saving, then so be it – and you can ignore this as the ravings of a mad woman who misses a life with supportive female companionship.

I believe our fallout and your fight (and what a fun one it was in retrospect – sorry!) had more underlying reasons than just the fact that I employed a white woman as a maid. I am therefore going to try for much needed candour.

I am aware, for my part, that I often let the two of you fight my wars for me. I do this by not expressing what it is I really feel about certain situations to either of you. Instead, I express this to a third party in the offending party's absence. This is how both of you can tell what offends me, and you often fight on my behalf. I have not been fair to you.

Moreover, since I am being candid here, I have to admit to you that although Marita is now invaluable to me as domestic help, I initially hired her to gauge Lauren's reaction. The fact that I was trying to bait you, Lauren, is inexcusable and for this I apologise profusely. However, now that she is working for me (hopefully for a long time to come), I hope you will be able to overlook her race and accord her the same treatment you, Lauren, would give any other person, race regardless.

I promise that I will try my best to be more honest with both of you whenever I am unhappy about anything. So here goes. Lauren: The way you treat MaRosie bothers me immensely (and I am sure I speak for Nosizwe too). While Siz and I are privileged black people, we still respect her by *virtue of her age as our culture requires, and we hope you can show her the same respect as you accord Ma, not overlooking, of course, the fact that she is a paid employee. I say this particularly having seen that you show deference to poor older white people. I am also uncomfortable with the gross generalisations you sometimes make regarding black people and how, when I challenge you with examples of Siz and myself, you say we are exceptions to the rule. There are a lot of people like us where we come from. Just as there are plenty of people like you who pulled themselves up by their bootstraps and are now successful.*

Nosizwe: You often bash on Lauren and her whiteness. I know you and I used to enjoy quoting Aggrey of Africa when we were in the Black Students' Union back in college:

If I died and went to heaven and God asked me would I like to be sent back to earth as a white man, I would say 'no'. Make me as black as you can and send me back.

Yes, you and I love our blackness, are proud of it as only a people long denied their heritage can be, BUT Lauren need not apologise for being white. She did not choose it – just as we did not choose to be black. OR female. We are what we are by accident of birth or, if you and I were religious we'd say, 'by the grace of God'. You and I had a more privileged upbringing than Lauren. While some white people in South Africa slaughtered and abused our people and benefited from the rights that the apartheid era gave them, Lauren was as young as we were and she is trying to survive and leave her legacy like all of us in the new, yet old, South Africa. Let you and I not hold Lauren responsible for all the follies of white people from slavery through the renaming of Mosi oa Tunya – just as Lauren, you should not hold all black people responsible for the church slayings and the car-jackings that some black people do. We should be able to watch a documentary of the ills of society and just realise that wrong is wrong whether it is perpetrated by black or white without getting offensive or defensive.

I know the demographics of our country are such that, Lauren, you still cannot go with Siz and I to Soweto without people referring to you as 'Nosizwe and Thandile's white friend', and we cannot go with you to some of your colleagues' parties without being referred to as 'Lauren's black friends'. Our country may be one nation but we are still different hues and shades and have our political biases laid on us by many years of apartheid but I truly feel, though we may not be able to change the country, we can change those who we come into contact with through our friendships and what we have learnt from each other.

I hope we all think about what I have said so that we can become better people. I miss you guys and hope you will be in touch soonest.

Much Love,
The Madam at # 279

Having completed the letter, I printed two copies, sealed them in envelopes and gave them to Marita to hand-deliver in the morning. She looked surprised, but not as surprised as Mandla, who has never ever known me to make concessions.

CHAPTER 8

Madam and Eve

On the Tuesday after the delivery of my letter, it became evident that I could not do without Marita.

I was sitting in a tedious financial-planning meeting when I received a frantic phone call from my son. He sounded as though he was in tears. I asked the number cruncher to excuse me from my office and he stepped out with what I thought was a 'can't trust a woman to do a man's job' look. I didn't care. I was worried since my son was only allowed to call me at work in dire emergencies. 'What's wrong baby?'

The response: 'Marita hit me.'

What? What happened, baby? Can you hold on while I call Marita from another line?'

I was concerned, but I doubted Marita would have hit him for no reason. She loved that boy too much. When I dialed her cellphone number, she sounded calm, although she was probably a little frantic about the prospect of losing her job. I didn't beat around the bush. 'Did you hit Hintsa?'

'Ja,' she admitted. 'I gave him a smack on the bottom after he had been cheeky to me.' She sounded a little nervous, but I thought to myself, she may have killed her husband, but she doesn't seem like a violent person unless really incited, so I figured the beating had been administered for a good reason. She and I had never talked about disciplining Hintsa and I thought it would be a good idea to leave her on pins and needles for administering punishment without discussing it with me first. I told her we would discuss it when I got home, and told Hintsa the same thing when I got back on the line with him – although he vehemently defended his innocence. More than once I had chastised Hintsa to pick up after himself, something he did prior to Marita's arrival, but which had suddenly become too much of a job. Mandla was much to blame for his son becoming a *piccanin baas*. Once, when I told Hintsa to clean up his muddy shoes, his father, ignoring the rules of mother-son confrontation, butted in telling the boy to ask his mother what the point of employing a maid was. The son duly echoed his father's statement and received a talking to from his mother, but the damage may already have been done.

So I got home to a sulky five-year-old and a resolute-looking maid. I asked Hintsa to go to his room while I talked to Marita, never having been one to embarrass adults in front of children as this went against the pecking order in my household.

'So, would you like to tell me what happened?' I asked Marita. I did not object to my child getting the odd smack, but I did not want her to think she could do it regularly either, so I had to sound strict. She was probably questioning whether she would just be fired, or be fired and put in stocks on charges of child abuse. To her credit, only the ashen tone of her skin gave away her fear. When she responded, her voice was steady.

'MaHintsa, I picked him up from school and made him a sandwich, which he refused to eat because it was cut in squares and he wanted triangles. So I made him another sandwich, which I cut in triangles. When he finished eating he went and stood in the middle of the kitchen floor, which I had just finished polishing, and peed on the floor!'

I needed no more convincing, I was now definitely on Team Marita.

'Little brat!' I exclaimed, stifling an outraged giggle. 'What did you do?'

'I told him to clean it up.' I nodded encouragement. 'Then he tells me that I'm the one getting paid and I have to clean it up.'

I shook my head in disbelief. 'So I grabbed him, pulled his shorts down, and spanked him five times on the backside, one for each of his years,' she continued. 'After that I took a mop, put it in his hands and told him I would give him more if he didn't wipe the floor clean. He did it, but he was crying all the while and when he finished, that's when he called you.'

I was impressed. Had this been a play, I would have given Marita a standing ovation. As it was, I gave her a 'thank you', told her never to tolerate any insolence from the boy and called Hintsa over.

'Would you like to tell me why Marita spanked you?' I asked, kneeling down to his height and deceiving him into believing that I was on his side.

'I don't know, she just did.' He gave the dumb five-year-old response.

'Yeah baby, but I find it difficult to believe that she would hit you for no reason. Remember mommy knows everything and if mommy knows you are lying as she does right now, somebody won't be going to the Eastern Cape for holidays.' In his teenage years he would probably realise that mommy was just another doofus who didn't know anything, but at the age of five, it was easy to convince him of his mother's omnipotent mind.

'Mumble mumble,' he said.

'Sorry, what was that? Speak up, mommy didn't hear you.'

'I SAID I mumble mumble on the floor.'

'Baby, you did what on the floor now? Don't waste mommy's time, you know she has to make dinner.'

'Peed.'

'And why were you doing that when you know where the bathroom is?'

'Just because …'

'Just because? Okay sweetie, mommy is going to spank your bottom just because.'

'No please mommy, I am sorry,' the boy said with tears streaming down his face.

When I was a young girl, I found that if I tried hard enough and thought of something sad, I could always cry. I have been able to cry on cue ever since, and for this reason, tears do not move me – I know well enough that they are manipulating tools. It was no different with seeing my son's tears.

'No you are not sorry. Because if you were sorry, you would not be telling me, you would be telling Auntie Marita, aye?' I answered.

'Auntie Marita I am sorry,' he said pitifully.

She graciously accepted his apology, and he promised not to do it again and took his punishment like a little man – and this time, not a howl was heard.

From that day forth, Marita's word became law in our home, the Eve to my Madam if you will, and while Hintsa loved her, I can honestly say he accorded her more respect than he did his father after this episode.

I think it was from that day forth that I started questioning, like every madam since time immemorial, how it was that I had ever managed to make do without my maid. Madamhood and maidship aside, and in spite of being a lousy cook, Marita had become a very important component of our household.

CHAPTER 9

All Good?

Each day since I wrote the letter I came home hoping to find a response, and for five straight days ... nothing. I was beginning to feel a bit stupid for writing the letter. Maybe I had been too rash. Maybe I had been too candid. Maybe I should have just sent a short little note saying, 'whatever I did wrong, I am really sorry, please get in touch. I miss you both so much.' This was beginning to feel like high school, when I gave the cutest guy in my school district my number and he took three weeks to call me. (Of course, by the time he finally called and I learnt he really liked me but was very shy, I was no longer interested.)

Mandla was amused at my antics; he kept looking at the phone and lifting it to see whether it still had a ringing tone.

It looked like they were just ignoring me.

Just as I was giving up on them, early on Friday evening while I was preparing for a night of bowling with Mandla and Hintsa, I received a letter delivered by MaRosie. 'It is so good to see you MaHintsa,' said MaRosie happily.

I didn't even get a chance to ask her what she was happy about. She lowered her voice, '*Eish mntanami*, I am glad you wrote that letter because those two stubborn *meisies*, they would not have budged. I am glad you were the most grown-up of all of them.'

She handed me an envelope. I knew before I even opened it that it was good news from my erstwhile girlfriends. I was not wrong.

Lauren always claimed typewritten letters seemed impersonal so the letter had a personal touch written in her flowing cursive. It read:

Darling Thandi
Thank you for getting in touch. I did not know whether I could keep on the pretence of ignoring you when I have had so much to say to you. I have missed talking to you over the wall and although unlike you, I have had Siz to talk to, let me be honest, Siz is no Thandi ...

How sweet, I thought, getting a little misty-eyed.

In your letter you accused me of being a racist or, at best, classist, judging from the way I treat MaRosie. To be quite honest, I never really thought about my actions or the way they affected those around me. I believed I was simply giving my domestic help orders and I guess you called my bluff when you hired a white woman as your maid. I suppose, as a South African, because this is all that I have ever known, it has become ingrained in me that black people (please don't cringe, I am going for as much candour as you gave) are the servant classes. It may probably be different with you and Siz because your experience abroad permitted you to see maids/au pairs/nannies of all races. It has not been that way with me and I daresay, if you had grown up here in South Africa and stayed here all your life, you would find it difficult, be you black or white, to adjust to a white person as a domestic worker.

I found myself grudgingly nodding my head.

> *Now onto the matter of the 'silent treatment' from Siz*
> *and myself. Seriously darling, it was not supposed to last*
> *as long as it did but you know how things have a way of*
> *spiralling out of control. After you threw us out of your*
> *house, Siz and I were both muttering about how it was your*
> *fault, and you have to admit we were right. You hired Marita*
> *to antagonise me and because that was what caused the fight*
> *between Siz and myself, it was only fitting that we come*
> *to the root of the problem. YOU.*

Okay. Maybe she had a point. It was my fault that they
ended up fighting. I had hired Marita to gauge Lauren's
reaction and I had got my reaction. A whole month's worth
of it.

> *I know we both refused to talk to you the next day but*
> *we had both hoped you would continue begging and plead-*
> *ing until we agreed to forgive you. Had I, for one, known*
> *that you would go into a sulk, I would definitely have talked*
> *to you the very next day. It has been quite torturous having*
> *to listen to Siz's stories of how Lizwe thinks she is better*
> *than her, not to mention how she fails to get excited when*
> *I tell her that Elizabeth received an A in her Sotho class,*
> *something that I know only you as a mother can relate to*
> *and be excited about.*
> *We will see you tomorrow for brunch and I promise to*
> *bring some delectable peace offerings.*
> *I have missed you much.*

> *Your loving friend,*
> *Lauren*

From Siz there was no letter, but there was a phone call just as I was leaving the house with the boys for our night out.

'Hey you,' she said, as though we had not had a freeze out for a month. 'Got your letter, glad to see that you aren't sulking no more.' Typical. Even when we fought at university, Siz and I never apologised to each other. 'Are you still sulking?' was all we would say, then pick up right where we left off as if nothing had ever happened. Old habits die hard. Siz was proof of that.

'So how have your days been with Madam?' I was genuinely curious.

She laughed, 'Girrrl, am I so glad you wrote that letter because if I'd had to feign any more interest in the Royal family or had to listen to another quote from another dead white man I would soon have committed suicide!' Then seriously, 'And I really missed you. I need to talk to you.'

Shit, I thought to myself, does she know about her hubby's shenanigans? I tried to sound flippant, 'Okay Miss Thang. See you tomorrow at brunch, huh? The boys are waiting for me.'

Dammit, why must I be thrust in the middle of drama every time?

After a couple of weeks, which felt like years, behind the Iron Curtain of my friends' affection, Lauren and Siz finally came by on Saturday bearing their peace offerings – Siz with the usual alcoholic good news and Lauren with a home-made pizza. Upon their arrival, Mandla tactfully excused himself to go to Gold Reef City with the guys and the children. 'If you girls spill any blood make sure you wipe it off,' was his parting shot, to great laughter. My girls were back – with their sense of humour intact.

'Soooo,' drawled Lauren, 'you missed us hey?'

'Not more than you two cat fighters missed me, meowww,' I responded nonchalantly.

'Honestly, I missed you and I know Lauren did too,' said Siz, joining what became an impromptu group hug.

Lauren pulled away first. 'By the way, Thandi, when I first read your letter I found it quite infuriating. I seriously considered jumping over the wall to come and give you a piece of my mind.'

Siz and I looked at each other thinking, 'Lauren, jumping over the wall? Ha!' The amusement must have been written on both our faces because Lauren continued.

'I know what the two of you are thinking. But believe me, when I am cross I can bring out the athleticism. Siz, you should know ...'

Which brought back good-humoured talk of the fight and who could have won it.

Siz interjected. 'Vuyo stopped me from overreacting.' Hearing the name of Vuyo brought a sour note to the happy reunion. 'Bloody cheating bastard,' I muttered under my breath.

'What did you say?' asked Lauren, concern written on her face.

I didn't realise that I had said it aloud and quickly tried to cover up. 'Ladies, this bottle is almost finished and I haven't finished cooking, so let's open another bottle and raise a toast to being the very fabulous Madams of the East – Lombardy East.'

'Hear hear,' they both agreed, downing the last of the wine in their glasses and passing them to me for refills. It was great to have them back. Sure, we had our differences, some of which we would never resolve, but we were agreeing to disagree. My high school headmaster was right after all when he said there was power in the number three –

three sides to a triangle, a very solid structure; Father, Son and Holy Spirit; and now Thandi, Lauren and Nosizwe – except that our trinity was far from holy.

We ate, drank and were merry, except for the disturbing feelings not far from the surface regarding Vuyo's infidelity. I did what I normally do when I don't want to think too much – I got busy preparing a gourmet meal so that I could concentrate on the ingredients and not on Vuyo the Rat.

I took a momentary break from chopping to SMS my dad: *Old Timer. The girls and I are having brunch. Now that Siz and I are good, shall I tell her about Vuyo? Advise Mr Drum. BabyGirl*

He quickly responded: *Not a good idea. Better to hint and she finds out on her own. Big Daddy Drum.*

My dad, like Napoleon, was almost always right. Why didn't I think of that?

'Earth to Thandi ... hello?' cooed Siz from her perch at the kitchen counter.

'Yeah what's up?' I answered, still a little distracted.

'Girl are you having an affair, who are you so busy SMSing? Let's see what this is all about!'

The last thing I wanted was Siz seeing what my dad and I had been communicating about. I showed her the inbox, 'Girl, it's just my father. He was saying he is glad all is well again.' Then I quickly deleted the message to make sure Siz could not look at it.

I was not going to let Vuyo mess up our fun. On this day we were all happy, carefree and, for a few hours anyway, single and free to mingle. During the second bottle of wine we relived our heydays with musicians who had disappeared off the scene, for one reason or another: Hi-Five, Bon Jovi, Bobby Brown (before he was Bobby Houston), and of course, it would never be a South African gathering without Mango

Groove (courtesy of Siz) and Brenda (courtesy of Lauren).

'Hey Lo,' I called out to Lauren who was cracking us up with a *Running Man/Cabbage Patch*-combo dance move in the living room. 'Remember when you told us about your parents?'

'Yes?' Lauren's face was suddenly serious and she reluctantly slowed down the dancing.

'I know you talk all this jazz about having royal British blood yada yada, but could your blood in fact be royal Mandingo? Coz girl, you sure dance like you got some black in you!' I teased.

Lauren, Anglophile, English lecturer and now Queen of Wit responded in accented ghetto lingo, 'Girl, I know I ain't got black in me but am seriously considering having some later.' Lauren lightening up about race? That cracked us up for a good fifteen minutes.

'Hey, why don't we all go out tonight? Eff the men, eff the kids. Just us. Girls. Bonding,' I suddenly burst out.

'Girl that's the best idea you've come up with all month,' intoned Siz. She suggested we treat ourselves to some pampering first – manicures, pedicures and clothes shopping (there was a Versace dress she just had to wear). 'I'll just call my man and tell him to pick up Pertunia from her studies.'

Whoo, boy. If Siz knew what I knew, she wouldn't be putting the very willing lamb in the belly of the beast. As it was, Lauren came to the rescue. 'Actually girls, I don't think that's a good idea.' Our night out was not to be.

'Let me guess …' answered Siz, 'you have to ask Mike's permission first?'

'It has nothing to do with Mike and asking for permission,' Lauren snipped. 'My GP has told me I have high blood pressure and that I need to lose weight. Thandi, you are always complaining about your weight. Okay Siz, you're perfect, but you're outnumbered ... I was thinking a weekend at a spa with some health food and all might do you, me and Thandi some good.'

Damn, what happened to these girls while I was away, coming up with such good ideas? 'I am soo in. How about you Siz?'

'Definitely! Actually I have been a bit worried ...' she confided, 'I think I must be getting a little fat, because Vuyo doesn't seem to have the va-va-voom that he had before, and he's always finding an excuse not to shag.'

Alrighty then. So things were that hot between Vuyo and Pertunia. I had to say something, 'Girl, you look good as always. Isn't your man almost thirty? They do say that men are in their prime when they are twenty so maybe he is just over the hill.'

This was going to be hard. I could not be cooking gourmet meals every time I was with Siz, and I could not keep pretending all was well and good when my conscience was bugging me. Maybe I could hold on until our spa date and then give her a hint. I sure was not going to let adulterous Vuyo mess up my reunion with my friends. I felt like the selfish only child that I was.

CHAPTER 10

Secrets and Spas

I had a sinking feeling that all was not well when I overheard MaRosie talking to Marita over the wall. 'Junior's mother is going to another conference this weekend, so I will come back with you … And they are going to pay me extra for working the weekend. It's good, *ne?'*

'Ja, definitely. MaHintsa also won't be here, but Hintsa's father is taking him to Soweto, so if you want I can come help you clean up tomorrow. Is Pertunia going to meet us at Chicken Licken?'

MaRosie answered, '*Eish* no. That Pertunia, she is acting too big now. She said she is going to be with …' then MaRosie winked.

Oh damn. I wish I had not heard all that. So Vuyo and Pertunia would probably be spending the weekend all tangled up in Siz's bed. How was I going to enjoy myself? (I wasn't too concerned that Lauren had told her husband she was going to a Wits conference. I have lied to my spouse every now and again, so who was I to question?)

The girls were at my house promptly at nine – even Siz, who was usually late. She must have been really worried about the state of her sex life. We were all in tracksuits, Siz in a designer FUBU and Lauren and I in our Mr Price specials.

'Hey ladeez, instead of our having a convoy why don't we just take one car, Siz, how about yours?' I suggested.

'Fine with me, but y'all going to have to fight it out on who sits in front,' Siz answered.

'I suggest that Lo sits in front, so that we don't look like we are chauffeuring the madam!' I threw in. Good-humoured Lauren was only too happy to cooperate.

We entered the spa like the women on a serious 'get fit' mission that we were. 'Lauren party of three,' said Lauren when we arrived at reception, she being the one who made the booking and sounding like a school marm with her charges.

'Oh welcome, come this way,' the probably overpaid receptionist said in her saccharine-sweet voice, no doubt seeing 'money' on the two overweight chicks and one fit one in designer wear who could be convinced that she needed to be fitter. She lead us to a buff-looking Indian guy who would have done Bollywood proud. 'Let me introduce you to your host, Zunaid Patel.'

'Ladies,' he said, sounding just like the guru that he was advertised to be. 'At this spa, we believe that people are unfit and unhealthy because they do not love themselves. Our mission is to give you a holistic way of losing weight and staying healthy. We are going to start with routine yoga. This is something that you can do in your own homes and, if done with your partners, will improve your sex lives.' We nudged each other like high school girls as he beamed at us.

Zunaid continued, 'Then you will enjoy some pampering facials and massages after which, we will give you your first meal ...' He went on to explain the exercise and pampering routine for the rest of the weekend.

Sounded good. We got on with the yoga. This Zunaid guy could bend body parts that I did not know could be bent. He kept coming up to Lauren and helping her, even when it did not seem as though she needed any help. She, in turn, was flirting shamelessly with him. This was so unlike her. And it was really annoying of him to be focusing on Lauren alone when we were all paying him. I nudged Siz and whispered that we should leave or tell Lauren and Zunaid to get a room. She whispered back that I was obsessed with male attention.

When we went to the facials I asked Lauren, 'Hey Ms Happily Married, what was up with you and the sex god in there? Did you notice that, Siz, or was it just me?'

'I sure did,' said Siz lifting a cucumber from her eye, 'Lauren, what would Mike say?'

'I am married, I am not blind,' answered Lauren flippantly. 'And, anyway, fuck Mike. This is my weekend and I am allowed to appreciate nature's creations.'

Siz and I looked at each other and mouthed, 'Damn!', while trying not to crack our face masks.

It was lunch that led us to decide that this holistic, keep-fit spa-thing was not for us.

'Ladies, let me lead you to a table full of food guaranteed to get rid of those love handles,' said a smarmy-looking waiter. We were taken aback. I, for one, had a peek at myself in the glass door to see just how big those love handles were. Then he went on to dump three plates full of leaves – with no consolation of dressing – in front of us. We all looked at each other and, as one, said, 'HELL NO!' You would think at one thou five a night they would give you a meal. We only waited for Lauren to go and take Zunaid's number (because she thought she would 'still like him to teach me yoga' – yeah right) before we sneaked out, scared that some spa Nazi would come and force us back inside.

As soon as we hit the freeway we all burst out laughing. We felt like Two Fat Ladies and one Charlie's Angel making a run for it.

'Lauren, where the hell did you find out about that place?' I asked. 'One of my colleagues from work recommended it,' giggled Lauren, dabbing her eyes, 'I should have known that it would be no good because she is such a skinny thing who doesn't drink or smoke and is a vegetarian.'

Siz joined in, 'Thandi, you should have seen your face when the waiter gave us those plates. You were like "Tell me you are joking". '

'Girl I WAS thinking that. You can't mess with me and my meat, you know that. So what do we do now? Do we just go back home?'

Lauren quickly jumped in. 'Hell no. I suggest we get some rooms at Sun International then do some partying. We can go home tomorrow.'

I was more than a little surprised at Homebody Lauren. 'I am with that,' I said. 'Siz, how does that grab you?'

Siz answered in the affirmative, but suggested that we drive to her house first so she could pick up an outfit. I secretly hoped that we might find Pertunia and Vuyo busy getting it on at Siz's house so I would not have the burden of breaking the bad news to her. Unfortunately for me, they had kept to their normal Saturday schedules.

While we waited at Siz's house for her to get it together, Lauren called Sun International for two adjoining suites near Mandela Square, so we would be close to the shops.

'Hey Lauren, why is it that Mandela is the only black person you white folks are comfortable with naming anything after?' I joked.

'That's easy. Mandela never brought up BEE, he never says anything about Black Power and he never pulled all that Biko stuff about "Why are we using forks and knives when white people are at our table?"' Lauren responded.

From the bedroom Siz shouted, 'Don't worry Thandi. Lauren and her Mandela-loving people are going to get it together when my godson becomes president. When he does, he is going to name everything after Thandi and I, so Lauren, enjoy it while it lasts girl.'

Lauren found that hilarious and started laughing so hard tears were streaming down her face for the second time that day.

As we stepped out, feeling ten years younger and with no commitments, we all sang along to Temptations' 'My Girl'. There is nothing that is as much fun as shopping with the girls, particularly if you have the cash.

At one point Lauren came out of the dressing room wearing a bright, shimmery gown from neck to toe. The dress only added to her pallor and hugged her very curvaceous figure, showing all those love handles. 'And this?' she asked, seeking approval.

Siz and I looked at each other in horror. 'Girl, I know you ain't thinking of wearing THAT!' I said.

'Nuh-uh girl. That outfit just screams tacky. Auntie Siz says no. You need to stop wearing khakis and jeans so much – you see how fashion-challenged you've become?'

'Aw come on,' Lauren said, 'I think it's a beautiful dress. Look how it looks in the window.'

'Baby, that dress looks good in the window because it's on a stick model, not a full-figured babelicious chick with tits like yours,' Siz answered, diplomatically.

'And speaking of full-figured ... Lauren, do you know that my son compared you and your husband to Jack Sprat and his wife?' I was not allowing the moment to pass without sharing that one.

'You see now Thandi, that's the reason I am never going to vote for your son as president, no matter how many alcoholic beverages you ply me with before I visit the voting booth,' Lauren shot back.

'But my dear Lauren, surely you want leadership that's honest?' I answered, and by this time Siz was laughing so hard she was holding her stomach.

I found a beautiful sleeveless Sun God'dess for Lauren to try on instead, but she refused. 'Girl, why not?' I asked her. It looked like something that would look good on her.

'My arms are looking a little too flabby,' she answered. She seemed overly uncomfortable about it. I guess we all have our insecurities.

At the hotel we all took an hour's nap in preparation for a rough night of partying. Waking up after six, we took it upon ourselves to treat ourselves to dinner in the hotel before hitting Spiro's for some pre-clubbing drinks.

We were dressed to the nines. Being the darkest of us three, Siz has always looked good in white and she had rightly brought along her slinky white Chanel dress with a low-cut front and back. I was in a traffic-light red, show-stopping, 'J-Lo-cut' dress, and showing the world what I was working with. Lauren had finally settled on a black gown with some billowy sleeves that would hide what she thought were flabby arms, downplayed her size and yet showed her chest off to its greatest advantage.

We entered Spiro's like the beautiful women that we were, and for a moment I swear conversation stopped as the patrons paused to gaze at the African goddesses who had graced this ordinary Greek restaurant in Melville. Not long after we were seated, some twenty-five-year-old-looking chap sidled up to our table.

'Hey ladies. You are looking good today,' he said by way of introduction.

'And we know it,' answered Siz, who had zero tolerance for boys bearing lines. 'Hey, I am Nosizwe, what can we do for you?' I asked kindly, deliberately using Siz's name as we often did and glaring at Siz for her attitude. The boy may have been young, but he was kinda cute in that John Legend way.

'And I am Thandi,' said Siz with mock contrition. 'How are you?' Which left Lauren having to say her real name because she couldn't appropriate either of ours.

The young man introduced himself as Sipho then sat on the arm of the chair,which was evidently the best position for checking out our cleavages.

'Sipho? And aren't you the gift, but we still don't know what we can do for you – or is it something you can do for us?' Siz said, getting into the game and making the poor boy blush.

'Dunno,' he mumbled shyly, but gawking at her chest. 'Just wanted to tell you all that you look so lovely and wanted to give you an invite to a party.'

And I teased, 'So do you want one of them or both to come to the party?'

He gulped like a fish caught on a line. 'Huh?'

'She wants to know whether you want one or both of Thandi's breasts to come to the party?' said Lauren.

Poor boy. He wasn't going to win with three sassy and experienced women so on top of their game tonight. 'Here is the invite ladies,' he stammered. 'Hope we see you all tonight …' And then he rushed off.

I was sure it was one of those Jozi raves where most of the girls are under twenty-one, but it was a compliment to our mojo and, of course, to Clinique and Mac, which had managed to keep us looking so delicious that this young man thought we were young enough to attend a function with him and his friends.

We agreed that we might just drop by Sipho and his friends later, but for now we were thinking exotic Northeners, and the place to go would be Kilimanjaro, where it was highly unlikely we would meet anybody who knew us. (Although Nigerians went to Kilimanjaro, I knew I would never see Chukwu there – he was surprisingly cheap for an Igbo man and would never fish out more than twenty rand on cover charge. This probably explained why he dated township girls who would be content with a six pack of Smirnoff Spin and a ride in the passenger seat of his Beemer.)

'I think I will call Zunaid and invite him,' announced Lauren, much to our surprise.

Obviously having forgiven our spa desertion, Zunaid arrived shortly after us and before long he and Lauren were dancing so close together that a sheet of paper would have struggled to fall between them. In between dances, home-girl was also downing more than her fair share of alcohol.

'What do you think is wrong with her? I have never seen her like this before,' I asked Siz.

'I have no idea. Maybe she is having domestic issues like all of us. Maybe the marital bed has gone a little cold and she is exploring her sexuality. I can't say I blame her,' Siz answered.

'Hey, none of the serious talk. What say we get a drink and worry about our problems another day?' I said, trying to cheer her up.

'Sounds good to me,' Siz responded, already halfway to being sloshed.

'Siz, do you think we would be like Lauren if we had got married to the first men we met?' I wondered, watching Zunaid with his hands full of Lauren.

'Probably, but luckily we already did our slutting at college, far away from the parents … Do you remember how all the

African guys disliked you because you always used to date black Americans when we were in college?' Siz asked.

'Don't I know it? But remember what my take on it was? NEVER GO OVERSEAS TO EAT PAP AND WORS!' we both chorused amidst peals of laughter.

'But dammit girl, if pussy could talk yours would have some stories to tell,' Siz said.

'Oh please. How about you and all those Kenyan and Ghanaian boys? If Vuyo knew where you'd been your ass would still be single,' I answered.

Reminders of Vuyo the Rat pushed me to ask the bartender, 'Do you have Blue Curacao liqueur?'

'Yes … why?'

'And do you have pineapple juice?'

'Yes ma'am. But what would you like me to do with it?'

'Aren't you the cheeky bartender?' I smiled flirtatiously, and gave him the following recipe: 'Put two shots of Curacao, two shots of Smirnoff, some sweet and sour mix and some pineapple juice in a mixer. Shake it up and give the drinks to my friend and I.'

The bartender was impressed. He did as requested and placed the drinks in front of us. 'That tastes pretty good ma'am, what's it called?'

Siz answered for me, 'That, dear Mr Bartender, is a Blue Hawaii.' She took a sip. 'Hey Thandi, he did this almost as well as you.'

'What do you know, he had a good teacher,' I answered, finding a way to toot my own horn as usual.

It took some doing to detach a drunken Lauren from Zunaid, but eventually we dragged her dead weight to the car. After parking and before going upstairs we decided to use plastic power and put an extra night on the suites. Not because we were planning to be there for another twenty-four hours, but because we did not want to be told to get out at midday. We were thinking more of getting out in the late afternoon after a long day's sleep with 'Do Not Disturb' signs on the doors and an eventual good meal from room service. And we did just that.

CHAPTER 11

Guns without Roses

The following Monday and Tuesday were busy days at the office – or out of the office, if you will, since I spent them visiting some elderly ladies who needed pointers on setting up a Sotho cultural village in the Tshwane area. On Wednesday I was back in the office and, not wanting to burden myself with Vuyo's guilt any longer, I hoped this would be the day that it would all come tumbling down for Siz's adulterous husband and evil Pertunia-of-the-pert-tits. I called Siz under the pretence of playing love doctor for the broken-hearted, Sis Dolly. I hoped she would jump to the bait.

I got straight to the point by asking her whether she was busy.

'What's up? Are we doing a girl's lunch?' she asked, never one to say no to time away from her desk.

'Actually no …' I said hesitantly, knowing that was one sure way to make her curious.

'Then what?'

'Well, I've been thinking about what you were saying over the weekend.' I proceeded to ask her whether Vuyo was going home for lunch that day.

'Girl, you know he's been going home for lunch everyday of late …' she responded, then, somewhat suspiciously, 'Why?'

I knew Siz. I was not going to tell her why. I did not want to run the risk of being wrong and destroying our newly-repaired friendship. So I told her, nonchalantly, that I thought she should surprise him with a lunch-time quickie at home and try to bring the fire back into their relationship.

'You psycho you!' she gasped, then started laughing. 'Why didn't I think of that? I love you. You are a genius. Let me just dash to the mall and get some sexy lingerie then I can really surprise him.'

'Don't rush,' I cautioned. I wanted to make sure that if he was at it today he would be caught in the act. 'You know you can't come between a man and his food, so it's better to get there when he will have finished eating, but before he has left.' I hoped she was not going to hate me when she found out what she was going home to.

'And hey, Siz?' I added before hanging up.

'Yeah?'

'Call me and let me know whether it worked.' Just my way of telling her that Sis Dolly will be there for her.

I was relieved that she was going with my plan. It made it easier. Some may wonder why I didn't just tell Siz about her Snoop Vuyo-Dog of a man, but I have been in a situation like this with her before. When Siz loves, she is always in denial of her partner's faults. If I had told her of my suspicions, Siz, as is typical of most women in denial, would get jumpy and immediately call her husband who would of course deny it and pull the 'your friend wants me and is jealous of what we have, I've seen the way she looks at me' number. This would result in tension every time we were around each other, with Vuyo hating me for knowing his secret and for knowing that I detested his treatment of my friend. Siz would also have issues, thinking that I was trying to come between her and her good man and that her mother had put me up to this, so it was better she saw it all for herself.

I called Marita and asked her whether the spare bedroom was clean. She answered in the affirmative, then just to be sure that should disaster strike I would not have her and my son on my hands I said, 'Listen, why don't you take Hintsa for a movie after school?'

Never one to look a gift horse in the mouth, Marita agreed to an afternoon at the movies without question. I then proceeded to call Mandla to tell him about our prospective house guest. I knew what was was on the tip of his tongue, but all he said was, 'I hope you know what you are doing.' It pissed me off. Did men not know anything about loyalty in friendship? Would Mandla have kept quiet if Siz was doing the same thing to Vuyo?

We heard the full story from Siz later, once the blood had been cleared. Vuyo was all hot and heavy with Pertunia in the master bedroom when Siz walked in, finding them in a compromising position. They were naked as the day they were born, so Vuyo could not even pretend that Pertunia had passed out and he was giving her mouth to mouth. Pertunia started cowering, covering her breasts with her hands. Vuyo, initially speechless, started mumbling 'it's not what it looks like', while Siz just stared. They must have thought she was just going to leave and they could carry on because the two of them just stayed sitting on the bed without even attempting to dress.

They had seriously misjudged our Nosizwe. While the two adulterers seemed frozen in time, Siz walked to her closet, opened the safe, and pulled out her Magnum .44. (She had become a trained marksman after her mother insisted that she and Lizwe both learn to protect themselves from Joburg hijackers.) 'By this time,' she told us, 'Vuyo probably had an idea about what I was about to do because he kept whispering "baby please don't" as though what he had to say was worth anything any more.'

'You,' she said, pointing the gun at Pertunia, 'put on your clothes right now.' Pertunia scurried to put on her clothes. Vuyo attempted to do the same, but Siz pointed the gun at him saying, 'NO. You stay that way.'

At this point Vuyo was alternating between fear and bravado. 'Come on sweetheart, I am sorry. Please put that down, you don't want to do this, please baby don't.' To which Siz coolly answered, 'But I do, sweetie,' putting her finger to the trigger and dislodging a bullet which buried itself in the headboard close to Vuyo's head. At this point, Pertunia lay down on the floor, all her apartheid-era instincts coming into play.

'Baby you will lose your job … get arrested … think, baby, think,' stuttered Vuyo, now less confident that his wife would not fire again. Siz was beyond rational thinking, but his words must have penetrated her angry mind. She aimed the weapon at him and told him to get out. Evidently he did not believe she would actually do anything because he just sat there, naked, on the bed, obviously thinking she would get over her madness – but Vuyo had not bargained on the fury of a scorned woman. Nosizwe aimed carefully and shot him in the thigh, not too distant from his crotch. 'The warning shot', as she now calls it. It was then that Vuyo realised he was dealing with a woman from another planet and that that planet was not Venus, but more like Mars, home of the warring deity.

As she recounted the story to me later on (with some relish), Siz says she spotted real fear in the eyes of the former

Sun City inmate as he ran to his car and drove away stark naked – probably to Edenvale Hospital, where he would lie about someone having robbed him of his clothes.

Siz proceeded to tell Pertunia to pack her things, called the locksmiths to come and immediately change her locks, called the babymamas to tell them if they did not fetch their children from school they would sleep outside, set the alarm in her house and locked up before leaving for my house, via Park Station.

Siz waited for the maid-who-would-be-mistress to get on the 1800hrs City to City bus to East London. It appears that, insofar as this Jezebel of a maid was concerned, for once Nosizwe's mother had been right about darkies biting the hand that feeds them. And this was not limited to Pertunia, but also extended to Vuyo, who had thoroughly failed to do right by her in spite of her almost saintly generosity.

I had already arrived by the time Siz got to my house. I could tell she was exhausted, her face was pale and pinched and the vitality of the previous weekend had vanished. I thought she would just want to rest, so I made us two cups of rooibos, making sure that for once I actually put sugar in hers for the shock, and sat with her. I held her as she wept, letting her know that I was there for her. She swore she was done with men – a statement every woman has uttered more than once in times of heartbreak – and she asked me to go and call Lauren.

I yelled at Lauren over the wall and, five minutes later, she was there. It being a crisis, I also called Mandla and asked him to pick up enough Chinese for ten, including the kids, to which Lauren corrected me by yelling 'eleven'. Siz looked at me quizzically.

'Who is the eleventh person?' I asked Lauren.

'Why, MaRosie of course. She has to eat too. Unless she

doesn't want Chinese, she can always make pap but she's free to decide,' said Lauren nonchalantly. My dear, sweet, Caucasian sister had actually taken my letter to heart. I could not stop myself, in this tragic time, from noting that she was such a doll. 'You are so sweet. I love you!'

'Oh stop with your mushiness,' Lauren responded, more pleased than embarrassed.

Hintsa had gone to Marita's room to impose himself with his Playstation. This was alright as Marita (or Eve as the girls and I were now calling her after the 'little *baas'* experience) was overpaid anyway and could afford a few extra hours of babysitting. Siz asked Lauren and I straight out whether we had known about Vuyo and Pertunia.

I admitted everything. 'I got to know during our "little tiff", and that is what prompted me, in addition to missing the two of you of course, to try and patch things up so that I could let you in on it.'

Lauren was contrite. Mike had told her too. 'Mike kept telling me it was none of my business and that I should leave it alone. I wanted to tell you so many times,' sniffled Lauren, reaching into the almost-empty box of tissues next to Siz.

'I'm sorry too,' I added. 'It was killing me not to tell you. I should have told you as soon as we got together, but I selfishly wanted you to have one last good time with us and know that Lauren and I are always here for you.'

The comforted became the comforter as Siz held Lauren and me. 'Please don't cry Lo. It wasn't your fault. It's that man I married, not you …' spat Siz with so much venom that had Vuyo been there he would have burnt in shame.

'He was supposed to be my husband and my best friend and he goes and does this to me … and with my maid IN MY BED,' Siz said through her tears. 'Did he have to sink that low?' Siz kept repeating over and over, as Lauren and

I held her. We looked at each other over Siz's head and we nodded in understanding.

To tell the truth, Nosizwe seemed more bothered by the fact that her husband had cheated on her with a maid than that he had cheated on her at all. It brought out my friend's class biases in spite of all her attempts to treat Pertunia like everybody else. And I think we are all like that. Wouldn't I be more offended having my man cheat on me with someone I believed to be below me than if he cheated on me with someone of my social standing? Sure, being cheated on would hurt, but it would hurt just that much more if I knew it was some Joburg beer-swilling, no-degree, three-children-from-three-babydaddies-having woman. For shame!

'I am glad you're here with me,' said Siz softly as shock and anger eventually gave way to exhaustion. 'Darling, your magic with the Magnum will ensure we will always stay on your good side,' said Lauren. Even Siz couldn't help smiling.

The poor girl was so emotionally exhausted that she fell asleep before my husband arrived with the food. I knew how much of herself Siz had given to Vuyo and how much she had sacrificed to be with him. For once, I wished for something more than that I might lose a few kilos without starvation or submitting to the discipline of a gym. For once I hoped, more than anything, that Nosizwe would be alright.

CHAPTER 12

After the Winter

The next morning, Siz woke up full of fire and immediately made tracks back to her home. She refused my entreaties that she stay at my house for a little longer. 'I am not letting Vuyo's infidelity and my maid's deception run me out of my own home. I am going to burn my bedding, but other than that I am staying in my house and that's that!' Ever the professional she added, 'Besides, I need to change to go to work, I am not letting those two idiots wreck my career too.'

No argument would make her change her mind, so when she had left, I immediately got on the phone to Siz's sister, Lizwe, in Mdantsane. Siz could be very emotional and I did not want to risk her doing something she might regret later while alone.

'Hey sis, how are you?' I asked.

'Girl, I so could be better but I am sure you people in Jozi are worse because your "etiquette rules" would never allow you to call me before six in the morning. What's up?'

I looked at my watch. I'll be damned, it was early. 'Uh, I didn't realise … It's Siz,' I answered.

'Not more family drama, please ...' Liz sounded worried. 'What happened?' Sensing the strain in her voice, I told her it was nothing Lauren and I could not handle but, ever selfless, Lizwe insisted on hearing the reason for my call. 'What is going on with my sometimes sister?'

'*Eish*. It's heavy man,' I replied. Then I told her everything, between her punctuations of 'Ohmigod' and, any time I mentioned Vuyo's name, 'Effin bastard, mommy was right about him'.

She had a few things she had to tie down that side, but said she would come up for the weekend and asked if we could distract Siz in the evenings until then. (We surmised that the weekend would be when Siz would be most likely to feel Vuyo's absence and get miserable.) I told her we'd have dinner ready and waiting for her on Saturday.

Saturday took a long time coming and, when it did, Lauren and I arrived at Siz's house much earlier than the usual brunch time; we wanted to see that she was okay. We were quite surprised to find her already awake and busy boxing up Vuyo's things. 'What are you going to do with it all?' I asked her.

With a look that had as much venom as a mamba about to strike she answered, 'Get in my car, let's go for a ride and you will see.' We drove to Soweto but halfway there I had to swap seats with her because she was crying so hard and driving even harder – both Lauren and I feared our children would be orphaned.

We arrived in Zola, stopped outside Vuyo's mother's house, and Siz dumped all his odds and ends on the street without a word to any of its inhabitants. On hearing the sound of the car Vuyo's mother came out and tried to talk to her. '*Yini manje squeeza*? Come inside, let's talk about it.'

'*Hayi*, there is nothing I have to say to you. I know you

never wanted your son and me to be together. Well you know what? You and your daughters can now keep your philandering, no-degree-having, sleeping-with-a-maid, jail-bird of a bastard son,' Sizwe's voice was rising by the decibel with every word she spoke. 'Ha! The grandchildren I paid tuition for, your son's children that I fed, clothed and educated, well that was the last of it. Now all your daughters are going to have to learn to work for themselves, because I do not want anything to do with any of you people.'

Seeing that this was getting out of hand, Lauren and I got out of the car and dragged our friend away. '*Hayi nix* Siz, let this go. *Umaole* lady was not involved with this,' I said, pulling her to the car.

'Oh yes she was. If she had taught her bastard of a son to respect his wife and his marriage I would never have found him fucking that slut of a maid in my bed.'

Loxion crowds love drama, and by now quite a gathering was forming outside Vuyo's mother's house. Lauren and I were battling with a tiger, but eventually we managed to drag Siz to the car and shove her in the passenger seat. Lauren held Siz down while I ran to the driver's side, and then I held her down so she would not go back outside and cause more drama, while Lauren got in the back. I locked the doors and drove out of there like a woman possessed. By now Siz had quit fighting with Lauren and I and was crying hysterically. A safe distance from Vuyo's mother's house, I stopped the car so we could calm her down.

There was little talk as we made our way back to Lombardy East. Siz had refused my offer to have her stay at my house for as long as she needed. 'No girl, thanks though. I need my space and I need to start learning how to stay by myself.'

But she had more business to take care of first. On arrival at Siz's place more drama awaited. She went into her bedroom and came out dragging the mattress and the bedding. We watched silently – not quite sure whether to help or not – as she proceeded to take anything else that reminded her of Vuyo; the lingerie he had bought her, the cards he had given her for all their anniversaries. Siz, in a *Waiting to Exhale* moment, proceeded to set it all on fire. 'They were cheap anyway,' she said as she watched the flames. 'Besides, they are mine to burn because I am sure that in some rounda-bout way he used my money to buy them.'

'Siz come on, not the Frederick's of Hollywood lingerie!' I tried to dissuade her half-heartedly, half wishing I could take these sexy little titbits off her hands. But Lauren seemed to be more on her page than mine. 'Leave her. Siz, if it makes you feel better … do what you have to.' And then aside to me, 'It's actually quite therapeutic.' I wondered what she knew about therapy in burning things.

But when she came out with an armful of toys belong-ing to the junior Vuyos, I protested again. 'Come now Siz, you cannot blame the children for the sins of the father, you know better than that.' This only resulted in her turn-ing her venom on me.

'Did your husband cheat on you with your maid? Were you looking after his bastard children? Did you promise to love and cherish him in spite of being warned against it by your mother? Did you secretly call someone you knew to give him a job because you knew no one would give him a chance because of his prison record? Does his family think you are not good enough for him in spite of all you have done for him? I didn't think so. So Thandi, fuck off with your self-righteousness, because you have no fuckin' idea how I feel. I can burn anything I damn well please!'

After that all I could do was stay out of this sister's way and hum 'Burn baby burn' to myself. But she wasn't done with us. She turned to Lauren, 'And you! If you fuckin' repeat any of this to my mother, you can forget that you have a friend called Nosizwe, you hear me?'

'But Siz, don't you think your mother should know? She is on your side...'

'Lo. I said you are to shut it. I will tell my mother when and if I feel like it, and since I don't want her to tell me how right she was, that's NEVER. You keep your big mouth zipped. And that means you too Thandi. Don't you dare say anything to my sister.'

Aw shit!

'Um, Siz?' I said.

'Oh you big-mouthed bitch, don't tell me you've already told her?'

'Girl, you know you are Lizwe's only sister and in spite of your little differences, she can support you much better than either Lauren and I can because she loves you unconditionally. We chose to be friends with you because we like you, but she is your little sister.' I thought I had hit just the right melodramatic note. 'Besides, she's arriving this evening.'

'Fuck, Thandi! When will you learn to mind your own business? I can just see her and Ma busy talking about "how foolish I was in the first place". Ain't that the pits? Now I am going to have to try and act normal otherwise she will rush to spill everything to our mother about how broken I am.'

Breaking the tension, Lauren suggested we go and pick up something to eat for the sibling rivals. Mandla and Michael were really supportive when Lauren and I called home and told them we would be at Siz's till late. 'Yeah, sure,' was all they said. Maybe they were feeling guilty for, in effect, being party to the conspiracy to break Siz's heart.

Lizwe arrived in an airport rental car just as I was about

to bake some spicy potatoes from one of my father's SMS recipes. Her eyes were swollen, her face haggard and her shoulders were sagging. 'Child, you look worse than your sister and she is the one whose husband cheated on her. Have you been overworking yourself again with your community projects?' I put the baking pan down on the table to hug her.

'Thanks for that vote of confidence – here I was thinking I still looked sixteen.'

'Nah. Right now, you look more seventeen and unsure of life. Siz and Lauren are getting the guest room ready, why don't you go and say "hey"?'

'How is Siz doing anyhow?' she whispered.

'Girl, I will tell you about today's drama when we are all together. Meanwhile go and greet your two half-sisters in there,' I joked.

Lauren and Siz came in arm-in-arm. 'She doesn't need to come in and say "hello", we're here.' Lauren gave her a motherly embrace. 'Lizwe, your body is probably the envy of diet fanatics like Thandi, but personally I think you have lost weight, have you been eating enough?'

'Yeah *sis'wam*,' Siz kissed her affectionately, 'You look as if you are the married, infertile woman with a cheating husband that I am, instead of the happy singleton still staying with mommy that you are.' Even in the midst of a crisis, she couldn't resist sarcasm.

'Well, it's nice to feel so welcome from all of you,' Lizwe forced a laugh. 'I am well enough … but ladies, can I get a cold beer before you all start on me, please?'

'Lizwe, I always said that your living in Monti was so not good. You are the only one among us who drinks beer and cannot appreciate my cocktails. Shortage of wines in Mdantsane?' I asked.

'T, get me a beer before you start asking me silly questions. I drink beer because I am a woman of the people and
the people drink beer – not that any of you middle class
chicks would know anything about "the people". Besides,
why must I drink Blue Hawaiis and Manhattans when I am
neither in Honolulu nor New York?'

Siz joined in, 'Thandi, as much as I love your cocktails,
this time I must agree with my sister. Aren't there any African cocktails anyway?'

It was obvious we were all trying to avoid Vuyo discus-
sions until after Lizwe had had time to relax. 'Thandi, was
Siz as crazy in university as she is now with all this talk of
African cocktails?' enquired Lauren tactfully.

I recounted how, when Siz had arrived at my university,
I had been so excited to see another person from South Africa
… until I introduced her to the rest of the pan-African
students.

'We were at a party and there was this bi-racial guy from
New York there. His father was Jamaican and his mother was
all blue-eyed blonde, like you Lauren. I introduced him to Siz
and he put his hand out to shake hers and she looked at him
with disgust and said, "I don't know where that hand has
been, but I do know it's nowhere near Africa." I wanted the
ground to swallow me. He was very cool … "So it's like that
sista?" he says to her. Siz just gave him a cutting look and said,
"Unless my mother spent some time on the islands and forgot
to tell me, you no brother of mine." As you can imagine, that
was the end of my university career as Miss Congeniality.'

The girls all laughed and we carried on swapping university stories over sundowners and the smell of spices roast-
ing in the oven.

'So Lizwe, how is Ma?' I eventually asked.

'Apart from dissecting my life and telling you how I

married the wrong guy and I had all this Vuyo drama coming to me that is?' said poor-me Siz.

Lizwe ignored her. 'She sends her greetings.'

But Siz, who was now quite tipsy, was not going to be ignored that easily. 'Yeah, but I'm curious to hear her biting comments about my life. I am sure she thinks I deserved this because I "married beneath me".'

Lizwe decided to answer her and put it all to rest, 'Nosizwe, mommy loves you and this is breaking her heart. You well know part of the reason that she was so against Vuyo was because, in her own funny way, she thought she was protecting you. I can't quite explain, it's a mother thing. I know I sometimes become overly protective with my son and I know these two are the same with their children.'

Lauren and I nodded – but only for a moment before Siz flew into a rage. 'Oh so now it's not enough that you are all discussing me behind my back about my "unworthy" husband, but now you also have to remind me how I am unable to be a mother?' she blazed.

'Relax. No one is discussing you behind your back. We are on YOUR side. Mommy just wants to know that you are alright,' Lizwe answered patiently.

'Yeah right,' Siz responded with the recklessness that she probably felt, 'she wants to know I am alright just like she wanted to know I was alright when she was busy sending you thousands of dollars for your Manhattan apartment while I shared a bedsitter? She wants to know I am alright just like she did when she was visiting you and would book in at 21 for dinner while I was sharing a hot dog with Thandi in Hawaii. She wants to know I am alright just like when I could not afford to go to graduate school and yet she had no problem paying for your tuition for SEVEN years of undergrad? Huh!'

Whoa. Obviously Siz had a lot of anger in her. And Lizwe was losing patience, 'Yeah, Ma was wrong Siz, but she is actually quite human and makes mistakes like all of us. She cares and maybe expects so much of you because she knows you have so much potential.'

'So that's what she calls it now, is it? You know, little sister, you can never understand how I feel because you have always had it easy. Vuyo was the one person who I thought I had to myself but, of course, with my luck, it turns out he wants my maid instead. But,' she shrugged her shoulders, 'you will never know what it's like to lose somebody you love, will you? Your life is perfect. You have a son that Ma loves and wants to stay with. The father of your child was gagging to marry you but you wanted your independence. You make me want to throw up.'

Lauren and I had been looking at Siz and Lizwe back and forth as this sibling rivalry tennis match went, so we didn't miss the moment when Lizwe's face changed. You could see her features snapping with impatience. 'I will never know what it's like to lose someone I love?' she said softly, shaking her head. 'I WILL NEVER KNOW WHAT IT'S LIKE TO LOSE SOMEONE I LOVE, YOU SAY?' she suddenly yelled. 'Siz you are so effin' busy feeling sorry for yourself, you are so selfish and wrapped up in your own life … which is why I never told you.' She gave a grim and humourless laugh. 'Ma and Pa are dying. I've been having sleepless nights nursing either one or the other. One of the parents who brought you up has full-blown Aids, and the woman who gave birth to you is HIV-positive. I've been watching them fade before my eyes daily. I don't know what it is like to lose someone I love? You're a piece of work, Nosizwe. You really are.'

Well, that got all of us sobered up. We just sat there, mouths agape.

Nosizwe, who had just downed her glass of wine, flinched as though she had been slapped, then hurled the glass against the wall and started crying.

The unasked question that hovered over our minds was the same: How? Who had given whom the virus?

'I thought this was a disease that struck younger people … teenagers, young adults …' Lauren spoke first.

'Was Ma's husband playing around a-la-Vuyo and put Ma on Death Row?' demanded Siz.

'Could there have been some doctor who was jealous of their success and gave them a bad transfusion?' I asked, ever the Queen of the Conspiracy Theory. And mentally I caught myself asking, if they had got it the traditional way, weren't they too old to be 'doing it' anyway?

Turns out Lizwe had asked herself many of the same questions, but even she didn't know the answer.

We absorbed the news in silence. 'So what's going to happen now?' I eventually asked.

Lizwe, the youngest yet the strongest of us all, informed us that Ma was planning on coming to Johannesburg as soon as she felt a bit stronger. She was already taking anti-retrovirals but, being Ma, she had decided she didn't like her doctor and wanted to be close to her favourite medicine men, Mandla and Chukwu, as well as take advantage of Jozi's excellent treatment facilities. Lizwe was returning to eMonti to look after Pa because, as she told it, he had been told by his doctor that he had left it too late and may be better off in a hospice.

Tentatively, Lizwe informed us that Ma had said she wanted to stay with Mandla and myself. 'She thinks it will be easier for her from Thandi's house since, as you know, Chukwu is her favourite doctor and what with Mandla being here and all, she thought it might ...' She turned to Siz, 'You don't mind do you?'

A contrite Siz answered, 'Of course not. It's fine. Please tell her to come soon. In fact Lizwe, please can you go back tomorrow, I feel very selfish having you here when Ma and Pa are both unwell.'

'Yeah,' Lauren added, 'we can all take care of each other this side. Oh my God ... why?' We all held each other, silently saying words to unknown deities, and when we disengaged, passed the box of Kleenex and opened a bottle of wine, which was shared in a sombre mood. Lizwe flew out the next day and we all, in our ways, prepared ourselves for the arrival Ma.

CHAPTER 13

Stronger Together?

There was an unexpected outcome from the tragedy of Ma's illness: it opened up a gap for the return of Vuyo.

Leaving his children with his mother, Vuyo was making regular trips to Mandla's surgery, ostensibly to check on what he thought was a hatchet job on stitching his bullet wound at Edenvale Hospital, but probably to get an insight of what was happening in his old world. Of course, Mandla filled me in on the events.

On leaving the Edenvale Hospital, Vuyo had gone to his mother's house where, Mandla told me, he was met with sympathy from his family on how wrong his union with that Model-C girl had been anyway and an 'I-told-you-so' or four from his mother.

Unfortunately for Vuyo's family, however wrong or right his union with Siz might have been, he was no longer accustomed to *loxion* girls whose only ambition, he would tell Mandla when he went limping into the surgery, was to ensure that the man they were talking to would be able to buy them their next quart of Hansa. 'Man I fucked up,' he would whine to Mandla. 'I miss her intellect, her sense of humour. I miss the way she knows what she wants from life, and the way she loves so unconditionally. I met an ex last week and tried to engage her in conversation about something I had seen on BBC news, but she had no idea what I was talking about.' This of course was all said in the hope that Mandla would repeat it to me and I would repeat it to Siz, and I knew this, but I was not getting involved in case he dogged her again.

They say love can conquer all, and in the case of Siz and Vuyo it did. Mandla told me how broken Vuyo was when he told him about Ma. 'Babes, he was torn. He knows Siz's mother doesn't like him but he keeps saying, "I messed up. I want to be there for Siz." He knows that it has to be difficult for her.'

To which I answered, 'Yeah right.'

But what Vuyo felt for Siz was obviously stronger than my cynicism, because not long after he heard the news, he managed to get some *cajones* and go and meet Siz personally. Knowing as he did that Siz was a person who did not like scenes (in spite of the one she had caused at his mother's house), he decided to make sure she heard him out by pitching up at her office without prior notice. The best and worst thing about her office was that it was open-plan so she could not very well raise her voice and yell, no matter how she felt.

I am not sure that Siz would have taken him back were it not for two reasons. Lauren and I had pointed out her first mistake to her: When she got married to Vuyo, wearing the rose-coloured glasses of love, believing in the 'happily ever after' and maybe also wanting to defy Ma, she married in community of property. Although the community consisted of her, Vuyo, his children and his extended family, the property belonged solely to her and if she divorced him, as she had considered doing, she would have to split all her assets in half. The second reason was that, in spite of Pertunia, the shooting, the drama at Vuyo's mother's house, and all the missteps that had occurred, Vuyo and Siz truly loved each other. The way she later told us, 'When I saw Vuyo enter my office, I just ran to him and we hugged each other the way they do in the movies.'

Whatever, but at least Siz was no longer wearing rose-coloured glasses. Having been bitten once, she had come to an important conclusion: this time, their relationship would be run by her rules. Vuyo had destroyed the trust that was the fabric of their relationship and for this he had to pay. He would have to prove that it was only her he wanted if they were to be together again. The reunion turned the split in Siz's favour because this time around, there was much negotiation and many visits to lawyers for Siz to draw up a post-marital agreement, which Vuyo dutifully signed.

And so he returned from his mother's abode to the bourgeois bosom of braais, expensive restaurants and indoor toilets in Lombardy East. It had been a cold winter for both of them, but now they could feel the tentative rays of a breaking spring together and, to us observers, they seemed more in love than they had ever been – with Vuyo in no doubt as to who was in the driver's seat of this relationship.

It took a little longer for Lauren and me to forgive Vuyo, but knowing that he needed our support, he invited Lauren and me to lunch one Saturday afternoon. We were wary. After all, we were very protective of our sisterfriend, but for the sake of Siz, we went.

'Yes. What is it?' challenged Lauren, the moment we had all sat down.

Vuyo started apologising, but Lauren was not going to let him off the hook so easily. After all, we were the ones who were left holding the dirty Kleenex after his infidelity. She wanted to know *exactly* what he was apologising for. He went on about how he had betrayed his wife, how he knew how much we cared for her and how her knowing we were not impressed with him was causing friction.

'I was just a fool and the moment Siz found me, I felt like death. I deserved her shooting me and I swear, I will never, ever do such a thing again!' While he said this he was rubbing the wound on his thigh – a reminder if ever there was one.

But Lauren wasn't done with him. 'All I want to know is, in light of what happened with Ma, did you at least have safe sex with Pertunia?' Lauren pried. Looking sheepish Vuyo answered, 'I was reckless. I am sorry. But when I got tested it was negative and Siz and I have agreed to use protection until after the window period, when I can get tested again.'

Here was Vuyo telling us he messed up, and all the textbook stuff that errant husbands have said to their faithful wives over the years. We weren't married to Vuyo, so we should have just looked at each other and him and said, 'Yeah, whatever,' but both Lauren and I were suckers for romance. And come on, how many times does your friend's man apologise to you for messing up your friend?

'Thanks for inviting us Vuyo,' I said on behalf of Lauren and myself, 'but what happens between Siz and you is strictly your business. I can't say that we are over the moon about your reunion, but if Siz is happy that is all that matters. Regarding your future treatment of her ... we'll see. Can we safely leave it at that?'

'No we cannot. You both do not have to love me. But I know you have been avoiding coming to our house since I returned and I just want to say that you don't have to be my friends, but please stop punishing Siz for taking me back – and trying to make our marriage work – by not visiting. She is lost without you guys. She needs all of our support with what's going on with her parents, you know that.'

'Ooh that is soo sweet,' cooed Lauren, and even I felt a little misty-eyed. Which is not the reaction we had planned to give Vuyo, but there it was.

CHAPTER 14

Drama on Woodward Street

Meantime, as is typical of Gauteng summers, a storm was brewing in quarters unknown to Siz and me. One Sunday afternoon, while Mandla was at his mother's house and I lay on the living room floor with Hintsa pretending that he was beating me at draughts, there was a violent knock on my front door.

I made my way slowly to the door, wondering what kind of salesperson works on a Sunday afternoon. The slower I walked the more insistent the knocking became and by the time I got to the door, I had some choice words for whoever was knocking. 'What the … ?'

There on the other side of the door was Lauren's first-born son, thirteen-year-old Junior, with tears streaming down his face. He seemed unable to talk and just pulled at my dress, indicating that I should follow him. I stopped him and tried to ask what was wrong. 'He is doing it again. He's going to kill her, please Aunt Thandi hurry up and do something.'

I had no idea who was doing what to whom, but I owed it to whomever it was to do what I could – and keep my conscience clear of a murder. So I let the boy drag me by the hand into Lauren's yard. There I came across a spectacle that I hope to high heavens I never live to see again.

A drunk Michael was kicking Lauren and bending down now and again to hit her with the empty whisky bottle in his hand while yelling, between blows, 'Bitch! You sleeping around with your slutty friends? You don't lie to me you dumb, fat slut. I will kill you.'

Meanwhile Lauren was ineffectually waving her arms about, in a vain attempt to protect herself. She was heavily bruised and there was blood streaming from somewhere, I could not tell where. I have never felt such fury in my life, I felt as though each blow Lauren was receiving was aimed at me. I do not know whether it was a case of violence begetting violence, but I grabbed the nearest thing, a Piki Tup trash can lid, as it happens, and bashed Mike on the head with all the strength I could muster. As soon as he was down, I started kicking him with what I now believe may have been the same fury that he had been using to kick Lauren a minute earlier, except mine was sober fury and therefore the blows landed better. I had the surprise element in my corner because when I started beating him, Mike had a 'what-the-fuck?' look on his face.

'Stop, Thandi. Stop. You are going to kill him,' Lauren yelled at me, and it finally penetrated the foggy parts of my mind that I was also partaking in violence. As Lauren stood up I noticed where the blood was coming from. She had a nasty cut on her eye from where his wedding ring had connected with her brow. One of her front teeth had also become dislodged from her mouth, her blouse was torn and there were bruises covering her arms and legs.

'God Lauren, how are you going to go to work in this state?' I asked and almost kicked myself as soon as the words were out of my mouth, because I sounded like the workaholic that I am. How could I be so stupid? More worried about her going to work than that she was okay ...

Michael, in his drunken stupor, was now snoring on the lawn where a few minutes before, he had been busy administering a beating. I took advantage of this and dragged Lauren, against her protests of wanting to nurse the abuser, to my house with her children in tow. I wanted to stop only briefly to check on the presence of my maid to look after the children. After taking Lauren to the hospital, I thought it would be safer to go to Siz's house as she was some distance away, in case Mike decided to follow and cause havoc. It was Marita's day off, but this was an emergency situation I thought she would understand.

A former victim of abuse herself, Marita immediately went into take-charge mode, telling me to take Lauren somewhere safe and offering to look after the children until further notice.

In between giving me orders on what to do, Marita kept shaking her head and voicing the old clichés of abusive men supposedly being from the lower classes, 'How could he? I thought he was educated.'

Fearing for the children's safety, I called a breathless-sounding Mandla and ordered him to come home immediately. Then, driving as if a Jehovah's Witness intent on converting me was on my tail, I rushed Lauren to Edenvale Hospital.

Between the Saturday night drunks, the drunk-driving accidents, and the victims of domestic violence from drunken husbands and lovers, Lauren and I had a long stay in the waiting room.

This gave me a chance to call Siz and brief her on the day's occurrences. Big-hearted Siz immediately told me to bring Lauren to her house for safety and despatched Vuyo to the mall to buy some toiletries and clothes for her to change into.

It was only once we were back at Siz's house and the tea had been made that we got the whole story. Speaking haltingly, in between tears, she told us something that, in retrospect, we should have been aware of: 'Mike has been beating me for most of our relationship.'

'What?' Siz and I both looked at her in horror.

'It began not long after we started dating at university. One day at the campus pub, I sat drinking with one of Mike's friends while he was playing pool and some guy came and started having a conversation with us. It was all quite innocent, but Mike came and dragged me off by the roots of my hair. As a sign of the times, none of the people who were in there did anything. The guy tried to tell Mike that he was just chatting, but his interference seemed to anger Mike even more and he just dragged me home.'

Lauren looked exhausted, so Siz and I stretched her out on the living room couch, covered her with a blanket, and we sat on the floor. (I was secretly thankful that the couch was coffee-coloured and as such the blood stains would not show.) Tired or not, she obviously needed to let go of almost two decades of abuse, because she continued, pausing only to take a sip of the by now lukewarm, sweet tea.

'When we moved into the flat, he really started beating me up. He always made sure he avoided the places that would be uncovered when I dressed. That has been his modus operandi until today when it seemed I pushed him a little further than normal, or he had drunk much more than normal, I don't know.'

'YOU PUSHED HIM TOO FAR?' Siz said. This was clearly an abused woman talking. Lauren was still blaming herself for the abuse ... and to think we had never known – all this time I had an abuser living next door!

'You don't understand. Michael always apologises every time he does it. I know he loves me and he says sometimes it's my fault, that I push him too far. He tells me it's because he loves me so much that he is so passionate towards me. He has promised not to do it again and he always cries, but maybe I cause him to hit me because, even if I stay cross at him for a while, I always realise that I may have been wrong and I forgive him. The truth is, when I received that first beating I was a little flattered as it showed he was jealous and still passionate about our relationship. I know he loves me.'

Twisted logic on Lauren's part or just masochism?

'No girl,' Siz wasn't mincing words, 'What he loves, evidently, is beating you!' Trying to come back to the present I asked, 'So what happened today?'

She recounted how Mike had been drinking since morning. He came into the kitchen as she was starting to make Sunday dinner and told her he knew there had been no Wits retreat the weekend we had all gone to the spa. Apparently he had overheard Marita and MaRosie talking about our spa visit. Damn maids. Maybe Lauren and I should have increased the height of our wall.

'He said he became suspicious,' she continued, somewhere between laughing and crying, 'and went and checked with the HOD for English, who told him we had not gone on any retreat. He said he has been quiet all this time, but today he wanted to teach me a lesson not to sleep around and lie to him. I told him I was just with you guys but he said you are both ball-busting bitches who would probably encourage me to sleep around because underneath it all you are probably dykes.'

Then she unbuttoned her long-sleeved denim shirt and showed us some of the old scars. I realised that in all the time we had been neighbours, I had never seen her in a bathing suit.

Siz and I had always perceived Mike to be the one put upon in the relationship. Had I not seen him hitting her, and had we not seen the bruises ourselves, we would have called any person who accused Mike of abuse a liar and maybe even accused them of defaming his character. In fact, we both would have been ready to testify, prior to this, that Michael was the most liberal of men, more of a feminist than most women.

It had been ingrained in Siz and I as we grew up that a man who beat up a woman was only half a man. We had also been taught that education contributed to 'civilisation' (whatever that is). We did not expect an educated, middle-class teacher, an imparter of knowledge to the impressionable youth to be beating up his wife – he was not some rural mine-worker à la *Yesterday*. Shows how little anyone knows about what goes on behind the closed doors of your neighbours' house.

When Lauren fell into a deep sleep, Siz and I talked further in the kitchen. We berated ourselves for not having noted anything untoward about Lauren and Mike's relationship.

'I cannot believe that we never noticed, and me living right next door to her,' I said.

'Yeah, but they both hid it so well, Thandi,' said Siz.

'But then again Siz, think about it … remember Lauren always used to pull the "I have to ask Mike" thing before we did anything?' I said, now seeing the obvious.

'Yeah, and you have seen how he always grabs on to her and orders her about when we are having braais. In retrospect T, we should have noticed. Shit, maybe Lizwe was right after all. I am a self-centred, selfish person.'

'No Siz. I was the bad one. I did not even notice and I

am right next-door. I am so consumed by my husband, my child and work.' Then I had a light-bulb Eureka moment. 'Siz! That's why she wanted a long-sleeved dress that spa weekend!' And, we realised, that was probably the reason Lauren had absolutely no problem flirting with Zunaid the masseur on that same weekend – she was hitting back the only way she knew how. Maybe she had secretly hoped that one of us would tell our husbands, who would eventually let her husband know.

'So what do we do Siz?' I asked, confused.

'Well, we can't let Lauren go back there, even if I have to keep her chained in this house for her own good. I know she has been taking this abuse for a long time but what would we do if he kills her next time?'

She was right of course. It was going to be difficult to help her break the chains that tied her to Michael but, if he killed her next time, we would be as responsible for her death as if we ourselves had struck the killing blow. We had to put a stop to it. Images of Mike as Joey Buttafuoco flooded my mind. No. We definitely could not let her go back.

When she woke up we continued with our line of questioning, but this time we were more focused. Had she ever laid charges against him for abuse?

'Of course I have. But I always dropped the charges after he apologised because he always told me I would be breaking up our family.' As if any child wants to live in an abusive family!

'Do you think,' I asked her gently, 'that maybe this time you could press charges and not drop them? Because you know hon, if you don't, and this happens again, he might kill you.' She refused. That is, until Vuyo returned from shopping.

He brought a mirror and showed her her face. She shivered at the first sight of herself – seeing the bruises that were fast becoming blue-black, the cut on the eye, the loose tooth. Then he did what we had not managed to do. He managed to get through to her by destroying the only defence she had for going back home to Mike – the 'father of my children' defence.

'Listen Lauren, if you go back there and Michael kills you next time, your children will be motherless and just as certainly fatherless, as I will either kill Mike myself or, if I don't, I will make sure he gets arrested. I will be a witness and make sure he stays in prison for a very long time. Is that what you want for your children?'

Lauren looked at him and visibly flinched, as if Vuyo had slapped her. Her eyes watered as she looked into the mirror. Vuyo, seeing he had made an impact continued authoritatively, 'You won't be doing your children any favours.'

Being a mother myself, I know that nothing beats a mother's love and Vuyo had stoked the fires. Lauren's anger at Mike came to the fore and she immediately became animated. 'You know what Vuyo? You are absolutely correct. Would you drive me to Orange Grove Police Station? I'm going to make sure that man gets arrested and charged,' Lauren's inner resolve was etched on her face as she spoke and we knew that she would not be going back to Mike.

The police promised to take Mike in that very same night. As soon as he was in custody, drunk and oblivious, Vuyo/ Prince Valiant drove Lauren home to pick up some clothing for her and her children, then came past my house to pick them up from Marita's loving custodial care.

Maybe it was the crisis, but Vuyo had become highly masterful and very likable, sexy as only a man in control can be. Upon his and Lauren's return, he called his immediate supervisor, telling him that he would not come in to work for the next two days. Siz did the same – citing a 'family emergency'. I never thought I would hear Siz refer to Lauren as family, but there it was. Lauren needed all the support she could get.

Vuyo gave orders in his masterful way, 'Listen honey. Tomorrow I will drop and pick up Lauren's kids from school. I would ask you to make breakfast for Lauren, but Lauren, you know my wife's cooking, so I'll pick you up some muffins if that's okay? Sweetheart, when I return from dropping the kids, we can take Lauren to the Domestic Violence Court in Market Street and get a restraining order against Mike.'

'But sweetie,' Siz interrupted, ever the independent married woman, 'I am sure that Lauren and I are capable of going to the court by ourselves.'

'I wouldn't advise it. You may need my protection. We don't know what Mike may try to do after spending a night in a holding cell. He might feel ready to show his vengeance to the woman and her meddlesome friends who he blames for his jail stint.'

Talking from experience? But I gave my tuppence, 'Vuyo is right. I have to agree there,' I said.

Lauren then called MaRosie who was at her sister's house in Alex and told her she could take the week off, paid of course, as no one was home. 'It's nothing serious,' she told MaRosie. 'We just needed to take a little trip so go ahead and spend some time with your sister.' We heard her answer on the speakerphone, '*Hawu*, thank you Madam. That is so sweet of you. Shoo, if I had known you would be giving me a paid week off I would have said an extra prayer in church for you today!'

Since Lauren had started treating her in a more humane way, MaRosie had become very affectionate towards her and the children. Had she known what had actually transpired, I would not have been surprised at her hiring some tsotsis to go and beat up Mike as he had beaten up his wife. By the end of the week, she would probably know through phone calls between her and Marita. I hoped, for Mike's sake, that he didn't ever run into her. I promised to send Mandla over as soon as he got home to check her stitches and give her some more painkillers. With Siz and Vuyo in charge, there was little else I could do.

CHAPTER 15

Whirlwind from the East

Mike was given a restraining order to stay away from Lauren and the kids, but that didn't stop him seeking full vengeance on the persons he thought responsible for destroying his happiness – Nosizwe and I. He went to Siz's workplace, walked in through the gate and flattened all four tyres on Siz's C200, which goes to show that when you are white and you are dressed nicely, security will let you go through anywhere in South Africa.

In a review of the security cameras later on, he was seen in action perpetrating the deed, cool as you please, without so much as a suspicious glance from the few people who passed by while he was doing his nasty work. Siz called me to tell me what had happened and I immediately made my way to her. I was, after all, the only person she could call on since her hubby was still at work and calling on Lauren would somehow have seemed like placing blame on her and highlighting the biggest mistake in her life.

Back at Siz's ranch, we had been inside less than an hour when Vuyo arrived.

'Let's go and press charges against that immature, woman-abusing half a man right now,' he said passionately, forgetting for a moment that the paint had not even dried on his new leaf post-Pertunia.

'That may be a bad idea,' said Siz, the voice of reason, 'he might do something worse.'

'I'm glad you are alright though, sweetie. Come here.' Vuyo spoke to his wife tenderly, and as she walked into his comforting arms, I took it as my cue to leave and crept out of their house.

Mike did something equally juvenile to Mandla and me. Entering into our yard through the servants' gate, which Marita had left open while she went to chat with MaRosie next door, he smashed a few windows and spray painted his name on the other panes. Fortunately for me and mine, we had burglar bars on the windows and as such, we could live a day or two without worrying about our security.

Lauren was taking strain. Particularly when she had to testify during Mike's domestic violence trial. He was found guilty and given a suspended sentence and a whopping fine, but by the time she got home, she would just lie on her bed and gaze at the ceiling like one possessed. Siz would call me often to come and join her in distracting Lauren with chit-chat.

We would be talking about all sorts of things to her and she would just keep quiet. Then, out of the blue, she would say something like 'You girls don't understand. He is an Arian and people born under the sign of Aries are very passionate, but I know he loves me and the children.' To which one of us would mumble, 'Of course you are right, hon,' while we looked at each other over her head with eyes that said, 'Your girl's going cuckoo.' But this, too, passed.

With our encouragement, the divorce was actually processed pretty quickly. It was a dirty divorce, but in the end she managed to find the one thing that she had lost, unknowingly, in all the time she had been with Michael – her self-respect and dignity.

Ever the strategist, Ma planned her trip to coincide with the end of Lauren's court case. Poor woman. She was always slim, but when she arrived Ma looked skeletal. In typical Ma style, she breezed in in the early hours of the evening without warning as we were preparing to sit down for dinner. 'Ma? Why didn't you call so that either Thandi or I could pick you up at the airport?' Mandla chided amidst hello hugs and kisses.

'I'm not an imbecile. I know the address of a house I've slept in millions of times, and I think I have enough money in my account to find R100 to pay for a taxi from Johannesburg Airport to Lombardy East. I am a little under the weather, some would say sick, but I am not poor,' she said emphatically. 'Besides, you probably wanted me to call you in advance so you children could prepare for me and pretend that all is good with the world – not likely. I am an African mother and I do not need to call to make an appointment with my own children before visiting them.' And that was that. The woman was incorrigible!

I busied myself setting an extra place at the table and Mandla carried her suitcase to the guest room where she would be parked for as long as she was going to be in Johannesburg for treatment. I was not worried about her settling in. Ma had a way of leaving her imprint on any place she entered in a way that would intimidate any person who did not know her well and even intimidated, every now and again, each and every one of us.

After sitting down, she called Hintsa. 'How is my second favourite grandchild? You have grown so much and in December you will come to the farm and milk the cows with Maqoma, yes?' she asked pinching his cheeks. Considering that she technically had only one grandchild in Lizwe's son, that was not much of a compliment, but Ma being the only grandmother Hintsa knew, he loved her as much as any grandchild can love his *makhulu*.

After dinner she got on the phone and summoned Siz and Lauren to my house. In the same commanding manner, it was she who took charge and sent Hintsa to bed.

'You are spoiling that boy rotten, a child his age should have been in bed over an hour ago. And he is a Leo, you know a lion needs a lot of sleep in order to be effective the next day. Now that I am here, things will change and no more of that American pseudo-physician Dr Seuss. I can't understand how two African parents cannot tell a child stories from our rich heritage, or at least some nice tales of King Arthur,' said the Anglophile *makhulu*.

When Hintsa was in bed, Ma started telling him stories of the warrior-king he was named after, and sang him some ancient Xhosa songs. It was then that she brought out the gift that she had brought for him – a hand-woven Xhosa shirt, designed by some of the women at a cultural village in Mthatha. 'Fit for a young man who has the name of a great chief, huh my boy?' she said, chucking him under the chin. Peeking in later, I noted that the boy slept hugging the shirt with a smile on his face, dreaming, I am sure, of the brave deeds his namesake had undertaken for the sake of his people in days past.

Vuyo came in with Siz to pay his respects to his mother-in-law (although he was probably uncertain how he would be received by that paradox of a woman). With everybody gathered, Ma commanded, 'Why don't you all sit down? I am sure you want to know what I have to say.' When Ma spoke like that, only a fool would dare to act in a contrary manner. We all sat. She looked at each and every one of us as though she were seeing us for the first time. We knew the routine, had been through it many a time. She was about to make comic fodder of us, as she did frequently, before embarking on any serious subject. Ma was renowned for her wicked sense of humour, but she was only funny when her barbed arrows were aimed at someone else and not you. We waited quietly and she, like a mean stage comedian, looked at each of us again to see who would be her first victim. Mandla, because he was looking down, and not at her, immediately lost.

'*Wena Mandla mfana*, better do something about that distasteful beard you are keeping. You look twenty years older than you are and I hear you have been drinking too much – I can see it from your gut. And what's this about the constant trips to Soweto during the weekend? Don't you know how to spend time with your wife and child any more?' Mandla knew better than to respond but did look daggers at me on hearing Ma mention the bit about too much drinking. I knew there would be some serious interrogation going on in the master bedroom after we turned in.

She turned to Lauren and complimented her, in a roundabout way, for finally kicking Michael to the curb. 'Don't look surprised you girls. I knew all along what was happening, but it is up to an individual to change his or her life. You can counsel all you want but it will do no good and sometimes it will even lead to resentment. Although, my dear, I don't know why you stuck with it for so long.' As Lauren's best friends, Siz and I should have been offended that Lauren had confided in Ma and not us but we were not. Although Ma was brutally honest and very judgmental, she had a way of listening and asking penetrating questions that made you confide in her even without planning to. (I think Lizwe has inherited this from her.) Should the Catholic Church ever choose to have lay priests who are female, Ma would make a great candidate for the confessional.

She returned to being light-hearted, this time to me, which did not bode well for Siz because it meant she was saving the best for last. 'Listen my baby, you have a pretty face, but have you been using that Virgin Active card you boast about, because you are looking a little too plump!'

'Actually mommy, I ain't been to the gym for a while, although what's sad is that Branson's empire suckered me into getting a gym card and to this day they are still getting my two-hundred rands every month.' She turned to Siz and Vuyo and, to our surprise, hugged both of them. She then looked at Vuyo intently and the confessor began to confess, 'Listen son. I have not always liked you. I never thought you were good enough for my baby. If you ever play around with my child again, I will come and haunt you from the grave for the rest of your days. Not that I plan to go any time soon, of course,' she said while gulping down the last bit of her orange juice. (In deference to Ma and more importantly because we were all shit-scared of her, we were laying off the alcoholic beverages on this, her first night.)

'I know you were all briefed by Lizwe about my HIV status. I am dying,' and here she lightened it up, 'as we all must, me maybe a little sooner than all of you because of this illness and my age, but what will be will be.

'Now I know you would like to hear more about my illness. Nosizwe, your sister tells me you have been going on with the "how did it happen" question?' Pause and deep breath. Truthfully we all wanted to know and we waited for it. 'I am going to tell all of you how I got it and I will tell you the same thing I told Lizwe when she asked me. In one word: sex. Now, I do not want to hear any more about this and we shall all go on with our lives without blaming anyone. Is that clear?'

It was clear. Ma had spoken. But she hadn't quite finished. She had more shocking news, but it had nothing to do with her illness. 'Vuyo, Pertunia is, as we speak, three months pregnant and I think you should consider going to the Eastern Cape and taking care of your responsibilities.'

We had hoped that the Vuyo-Pertunia saga had left Johannesburg when Pertunia boarded the City to City bus, but it seemed that now she would be a constant in Nosizwe's life, if only as an unfortunate reminder of her husband's infidelity. Vuyo jumped to sing that oh-so-famous International Men's Anthem of 'it wasn't me' but Nosizwe was quick. 'Shut up Vuyo. You know very well you weren't even wearing any protection.'

Ma continued as if she had not been interrupted, this time with a devious smile on her face, 'Nosizwe, I heard about the shooting and I am proud of you. Vuyo, you deserved it and if you should ever disrespect my daughter again, dead or alive, I will make sure you regret the day you were born and this time, it may be me holding the gun.'

She then got practical. 'Mandla, I will ask Dr Chukwu to consult with you on the best treatment options for me. I know your practice has been doing so much good work in HIV/Aids care and treatment and I have faith that I am in good hands. Naturally, I will buy my medication from your pharmacy to make sure that I am keeping the money in the family.' She said all this quite light-heartedly.

She then turned to Siz and Vuyo and told them that, having now blessed their union, she would have liked to stay with them but thought it better to stay with Mandla and me. 'I do not want you two children rushing me to the doctor when I can have an in-house one.'

She then commanded Mandla and me that we would have to ride to work together for a while as she was going to be using my car to get around, adding in an aside that it might be for the best since my bum was too big for that lovely car anyway. Vicious? I should think so. I said a tad emotionally, 'Ma, would you please stop with the big ass jokes?'

'*Haibo,*' she answered, 'you want me to stop, you go to the gym and do something about it, or *ndiyadlala* Mandla?'

Knowing who kept his bed warm, Mandla just shrugged. We were all grateful that she had reverted back to her old speech as it made it easier to deal with her illness. She had spoken bravely and I do not know whether there was ever a time when we loved Ma more than we all did on this occasion. I thought to myself that Ma had been short-changed by the generation she was born in. She was far ahead of her time and it was unfortunate that when she grew up, the only professions open to black women were nursing, teaching and social work. She would have made a brilliant advocate … I could not imagine her losing a debate.

CHAPTER 16

Rebirth and Reconciliation

In no time at all, it felt like Ma had always been a part of our household. Her presence had managed to change every individual in my little house, but we had been changed for the better.

Hintsa did his homework quicker because he wanted to be told stories about famous African warriors of days gone by, tales that Ma had plenty of. When Ma first met Marita, she immediately became her trade union representative. 'I hope these two are not exploiting you because if they are, here is the number for your local union.' That she had taken time to research that information before she came to Johannesburg was an indication of how Ma never left anything to chance, and Marita loved her for it. With the help of Ma, my maid was exercising her culinary skills and had even managed to make a successfull macaroni and cheese that the whole family enjoyed for dinner one night.

Mandla again became the charming man who courted me; he seemed to have more time to spend with his family, and would often come to my workplace at lunch time with a treat, or just call, 'to tell you I love you'. Ooh! 'So, are you trying to impress Ma or are you trying to impress me?' I asked him one day when he had brought me flowers. 'What happened to all that talk of "You are my wife now, I don't need to buy you flowers?"'

'That's the problem with you Thandi. Over analytical. Can't you just say, "Thanks babes, the flowers are lovely. Now since my PA is out, let's go lock ourselves in my office and I will show you just how grateful I am?"' he smirked, hopefully.

'What? And disillusion my PA when she returns because she will realise married people actually shag?' I returned.

At home we settled into a routine where Ma would wake up, give Hintsa his bath and breakfast and drive him to pre-school, returning home with the newspapers. While Marita was cleaning, Ma would peruse the papers for the zodiac predictions of the day, compile them, along with the most pressing current issues, send them to Marita for editing and email them to Siz, Mandla and myself before lunch time.

Ma, typically, had charmed Marita with her star-gazing predictions, 'You shouldn't have been with your late husband anyway. He was a Leo and you are a Cancer and everyone knows that fire and water don't mix. Next time you are interested in a young man, just call Ma and I will let you know whether it will work or whether you are just wasting your time,' I overheard Ma telling Marita. To which Marita responded, 'Ag, I think you are right, Ma. Lauren told me the same thing.'

Siz, Mandla and I did not believe in the whole zodiac thing as religiously as she and Lauren did, but we had begun to appreciate this labour of love and would attempt to be conversant with our star issues of the day to show our love at the dinner table. 'How was your day?' in my household was now answered by Mandla thus: 'Mars was in my sun sign, Sagittarius, which resulted in a fruitful day for me and

I attended to a record number of patients.' Not that I am sure whether Mandla really understood what either the Roman god of war or the planet closest to earth had to do with his daily fortunes, but it made Ma happy and we all became a little less selfish while she was there.

Every night from the time of her arrival, I started doing something that so-called atheists do in desperate times: I prayed.

'My Good Lady,' I said 'Yes, you they call God. I know what I have said about religion and you in conversation, but I am not asking this for me now, I'm asking for someone else so can you please heed my prayer, woman to woman? If you are really, really there, please help Ma. Help some scientist out there find the cure for this dreaded illness that's taking our youth in their prime, and our adults when they should be enjoying their twilight years. Sorry again, and please don't hold my words and actions against Ma, but help that sister out if you can. After all, shouldn't girls be looking out for each other God girl?' If God was a woman I was sure this prayer would make her help Ma out but if the deity was male, I crossed my fingers and hoped that he was humorous enough to be cool with my seeing him in my own image.

I concluded that God was a woman because within two months Ma's CD4 count went up from 120 to over 500. And because when a door closes She opens a window, God achieved another coup. Without the shadow of Lizwe, and therefore no petty jealousies or over attentiveness to 'Ma's baby', Siz and Ma also attained a closeness they had never had before; a closeness based on mutual respect.

After Ma's lab tests and a month's monitoring, she left with Hintsa in tow for the December school holidays. We were sad to see her go, which was ironic, because a few months before you could never have convinced Siz or myself that we would be sad to see Ma leave the town we inhabited.

Marita came to me one day, with that look unique to maids the world over when they want something but want you to pry it out of them.

'You look really lovely with your hair like that MaHintsa,' she began.

'Yeah yeah, I know you want something so get on with it and tell me what it is,' I teased.

Then Marita, all serious said, 'One of my old prison mates has invited me to Soweto for the holiday season, and since I haven't taken any time off from work yet, I was wondering whether I could leave for a month. I'm not trying to be ungrateful and if you don't want me to go I will stay, you know, but I thought since Hintsa ...'

'STOP!' I interrupted because I could see this was going to take a very long time, 'Yes, you can go. Tomorrow if you want, I just need to dash to the bank so that I can give you a little extra.'

As testament to our nation's mentality, I was rather surprised to see a white woman, maid or not, who wanted to spend a whole month's holiday in Soweto so I asked her, 'Soweto's a bit of a surprise though?'

'My, um ... Mary used to say when we were in prison that black people know so much about us but we don't seem to want to really know about them, and we can never truly reconcile if we do not meet them halfway. I thought I would try to get to know what *loxion* life is like.'

My maid the sociologist was certainly crossing barriers as a white woman in South Africa. I told her I hoped she would find the experience enlightening.

'I am sure I will. She said I could go see the Museums.

There's a new one called the Alf Kumalo Museum, have you been there? Mary says there's more photos there than all the others in Soweto and by one photographer, *nogal.'*

I laughed. 'Of course I've been there. Tourism is my job, remember? Alf probably has all that work because he has been a photographer since the Fifties. So what else are you planning with this Mary friend of yours?'

'We are also gonna jol, hey! She told me she will take me to The Rock, and then Mary likes her beer so we shall probably be there at shebeens. It's her house *mos*. Her parents left it for her so she said I can stay as long as I like.'

Then she did something rather untoward which had me feeling embarrassed; my maid came and gave me a warm resounding kiss to show her gratitude.

'Hey none of this mushy stuff. You might make me reconsider!' I said, trying to cover up how sweet I thought it was.

With the gate keys and her thirteenth cheque, Marita departed for Soweto and now it was just me and my husband in the yard.

Being the ultimate romantic that I am, covered in a layer of realism but always hoping, I took the absence of 'the staff' as a time to recapture the magic with my significant other. Mandla took it as time to re-bond with old drinking buddies and would come in, allegedly from drinking with the boys in Soweto, at all hours of the morning. Gone was the romance. 'What do you mean I don't spend time with you? I sleep beside you every night and I see you every day,' was the response I got one time when I questioned him about his absentee husband role.

Since my office was staying open until Reconciliation Day, I used that time to work later and longer hours, but if Mandla noticed this silent protest, he never mentioned it. For some unknown reason, no matter how late I stayed,

Mandla was always later. I started having my dinner daily at Lauren's house and only going to my house to sleep. If Mandla missed me, he never indicated it.

It was at this time that a ghost from our past reappeared: Michael.

Lauren told Siz and myself during one of our brunches that he had changed. 'After the divorce, he was staying in some sort of boarding house in town where he made some Muslim friends. He converted to Islam and his name is now Mohammed. Now he punctuates every statement with "Inshallah" and "Peace Be Upon Him".'

Apparently the children – with the exception of Junior – were initially happy to see him, but that changed. 'He seems keen to convert them and the other day he was telling me that my clothes are too revealing.' I looked at Lauren in her khakhis and long-sleeved checked shirt and burst out laughing.

Brother Mohammed sent Siz and I, via Lauren, long-winded notes about how sorry he was about the damage to our property, and how he had seen salvation and that we could call him any time for a tutorial on the Holy Koran so we too could learn the true way. 'Eish, I wish Brother Mohammed had sent some form of financial redress with his apology,' Siz said, 'I could have taken my godson shopping.'

After Michael left (he was now apparently residing in a sort of half-way house), we asked Lauren whether she was considering getting back together with Michael. 'So Lo,' I teased, 'are you planning to convert, quit your drinking habits and become Sister Khadija to Michael's Mohammed?'

Lauren's answer was a strong and emphatic 'Hell no, but I tell you what, I think I am going to call Zunaid the Yogi. I would like to be educated on how better to twist and bend certain body parts – if you know what I mean.' Having tasted independence, Lauren was not anxious to give it up just yet.

'You still have that guy's number?' Siz smiled. 'Well the good news is Brother Mohammed brought you religion, the bad news is, we are not sure whether he will be too pleased with the religion you have been awakened to.'

A few weeks later, while we were having a drink at Lauren's house, her third-born, Diana,came in holding something behind her back. 'Hey little princess, what you got there?'

I wanted to burst out laughing but had to keep a stern face. Lauren's daughter was holding a vibrator.

'Where did you get that?' I asked.

'Junior told me to look for a marker in mummy's drawer and I found this in there. What is it mummy?' asked the innocent.

Lauren jumped in cool as you please, 'It's a tool, my darling. See how it vibrates and lights up? Well, it's used when you are trying to make a hole in the wall and you want to see whether it's deep enough. Now go and put it back like a good girl.'

Her daughter did not seem entirely convinced with the explanation. I hoped it would be ages before she knew what it actually did! As soon as she was gone Lauren and I both burst out laughing. 'Girl, what the heck?' I asked her.

'I normally keep it in a suitcase on top of the cupboard, but Zunaid was over last night and after a particularly long yoga session I wasn't up to it putting it back.' My girl tells me this totally straight-faced.

'You? Zunaid? Since when? And what about the kids?' I bombarded her with questions.

'I called him and … well, he offered to give me some private yoga classes. I bet you didn't know I could do this,' she said kneeling and bending over backwards until her head touched the ground. 'And anyway, I am grown up and have my needs, and my kids also like Zunaid because he teaches them some neat yoga tricks.'

What more could I say but 'DAMN!' While married me was wondering 'when next?' with my man, Team Lauren was getting it on!

CHAPTER 17

Ghosts

Two days before Reconciliation Day, while in the office, I received a call from Lizwe. I heard her voice breaking from the other end.

'It's Pa. He's gone Thandi, about an hour ago,' she said.

'Does Siz know yet? Do you want me to tell her?' There was no time for me to be selfish and think of how I seemed, these days, always to be the bearer of bad news.

'Yes, thanks. How soon can you both get here?' she asked. 'Everything is upside down. Ma and I are running back and forth but we could really use your help.'

'Don't stress too much,' I answered, 'I will arrange with Siz and we can get on a flight today.' I was already looking for my credit card.

I made a phone call to my boss in Pretoria telling him that I had to take emergency leave, 'My grandfather died,' I lied. I didn't think God or the ancestors would punish me since I did not even know any of my grandfathers. Besides, they were white, and I'm not even sure white people have ancestors.

We arranged it so that Vuyo and Mandla would pack up and follow in two days. We knew full well that we, as women, would have a lot of work to do, hosting mourners and cleaning up the house. All that was expected of the men was to take part in rituals and, when the time came, to slaughter the beasts. That would only be done a day or two before the funeral so there was no rush on their part.

Lauren called MaRosie from her Christmas break (yes, Lauren had become the type of madam that the unions would award) to see whether she could come and babysit so she could attend the funeral. MaRosie, ever the loving woman, was happy to.

We all flew to East London where we were met by Lizwe at the landing pad that poses as an airport in that town. Making our way to Mdantsane, I made a mental note of the legacy of apartheid as I observed the well-maintained roads of the suburbs versus the dust roads that we would encounter in some of the side roads in the *loxion*.

'Ma, aren't you supposed to be on the mattress?' I asked Ma, who was busy giving orders back and forth and not chilling on a mattress like a bereaved widow, as our culture dictates we do.

'Child please, me on a mattress? I would die of boredom, besides I want to make sure those Zwelitsha women who claim they want to help don't end up putting the rice in their bags.' Damn!

When Lauren arrived she drew much amusement every time she tried to speak isiXhosa, and admiration from the elders for donning a doek and kneeling to serve the elderly, – often in the correct cultural order. Having black friends was certainly paying off.

'What are you complimenting her for?' Ma chided. 'Don't you know I taught all my children, including the white one, well? No one attends MaNdlovu's School and comes out short changed.' In a moment of light-heartedness, a couple of *malumes*, on hearing that Lauren was divorced with four children, started bantering and making requests for her hand in marriage, given that she could *hlonipha* and was fertile. By the end of the funeral everyone was referring to Lauren as MaDlamini because a certain relative whose clan name was Dlamini had informally adopted Lauren as his daughter. My dad also came down on the day of the funeral. I noticed that he spent hours laughing and whispering with Vuyo, then getting silent every time Mandla appeared. I called him to order, 'Daddy what do you think you are doing?'

'What are you talking about child? Is that how you speak to your father?' he asked.

'I see that you are ignoring Mandla every time he comes by. Daddy, he is my husband and related to you, stop doing that.'

My daddy gave me a humourless smile, 'Yes child. He is your husband, that he is. And a pompous ass, too. I am talking to Vuyo and he comes to start every sentence with "When I was in America". For crying out loud.'

I kissed my father. 'Be nice. We're at a funeral, okay?'

In so far as funerals can be said to be successful, Pa's funeral was just that. A Xhosa's funeral being determined by the meat available, Ma had purchased two cows for the occasion. In addition, there was a donation of sheep and goats from the ruling party to a fallen comrade. On the day of the funeral itself, many, including the premier, a few cabinet members and some members of parliament, graced the funeral. It was a fitting send-off for this man of high political ideals; this man who many had loved and respected but, at the end, could not save.

Such was life, as Ma was to be heard saying later on. In the end, no matter what ideals one had, we were all fallible, 'All things must come to dust.'

The only fly in the ointment at the funeral was the appearance of Pertunia. She (coincidentally?) appeared a few hours after the arrival of Vuyo and Mandla with her three children and her pregnancy. Ma, not wanting to dishonor the dead (or so she said), went to Pertunia's mother and said, '*MaPertunia, ndiyacela uchel'i umntwana lo* to please not cause any problems at my husband's funeral. Vuyo and Nosizwe are both here, we can talk about all this after the funeral, *ne?*'

A family court was thus convened the day after the burial, to discuss the problem of Pertunia's pregnancy with Nosizwe's husband. Vuyo asked my father to be present as a father figure.

Lauren and I stayed behind after the funeral so that we could be there for Siz for either some ass-kicking or moral-support. It was a woman's show, given that Siz's paternal family – aside from her uncle, who received the lobola – did not get along well with her mother, and Pertunia's mother was unmarried. The only men who were there were Pertunia's brother, Nosizwe's uncle, my father and Vuyo. Lauren, Lizwe and I brought in the tea and tried to get in under any pretext, so that we could see what was transpiring.

After one such episode, I came out and whispered to the other two, 'Eish. That place is damn tense. Siz looks like she is about to kick some serious Pertunia ass …'

After a while Ma, ever observant, decided to call us on our stupid tricks. She told Lizwe, who had supposedly gone to pick up the tea things, 'Hey, *uzaziyenzi uclevah*, you and those other two with your in-and-outs. Do you think I am so stupid I cannot notice that you *mamGobozis* are trying to hear what's going on? You can't wait for Siz to tell you her own stories herself?'

'Sorry *Mawee*,' answered a contrite Lizwe. Lauren and I

crept away from the window where we were standing so that we could hear the proceedings in shame. 'Ja. That's right,' we overheard Ma add as we slunk off, 'and if I see any of you in here again, I do not care how old you are or how old your child is, I will talk to you like the teenagers you are acting like.'

It was over three hours after Ma's reprimand that the party finally emerged from their closed-door session. As we had to serve them a late lunch, we had to wait another hour and a half before Siz came and told us the results of the discussion. We were around her like moths to a flame.

'So what happened?' Lauren asked. Siz looked like the outcome had worked in her favour. Our assumption was not far wrong. 'Now y'all know and I know that Vuyo would never abandon his children *nomakanjani*, so, instead of worrying about what might be happening every time he comes east to visit the child, I suggested that I adopt the child and bring it up as my own, since I can't have any children.'

Lauren, Lizwe and I gaped at each other. Hold up! This was the girl who only took in Vuyo's other two children because she was afraid that her man would go creeping back to his exes under the pretext of going to see his children. It was Lizwe who vocalised what we were all wondering.

'Excuse me my dear sister, but you didn't even like the other children that Vuyo already has.'

Then we heard Siz's side of the story.

Wringing her hands and looking like an insecure child she said, 'Thing is … I sometimes think that maybe Vuyo got with Pertunia because she was more maternal towards his children while I just ignored them. I need to show him that I am not just a selfish, spoilt rich girl. That I am capable of loving his child selflessly …' then grinning slyly, 'And of course the added bonus is that that Pertunia bitch will be losing the child she made under deception to me, but I didn't say that in there. What I said was that the child would be better off with us since Pertunia has no income.'

And Pertunia was okay with that? Evidently. Siz continued that the only sticking point had been Pertunia wanting to keep the child until she was a year old and Siz adamantly refusing. The compromise that was reached was more to Siz's than to Pertunia's liking. It was agreed that Siz would take the child from birth, but she could be brought east to visit at least once a year so she would know her biological mother. *Tsho*. It looks like the rich will always triumph over the poor.

Siz was sure she would love the child as though it were her own and, being the big-hearted character that she was, and with no annoying babymama constantly calling her landline, maybe this time it would work out for Siz. The battle lines between her and Pertunia had, however, been drawn. In her heart, Siz decided that the best revenge would be if Pertunia's child grew to love her foster mother more than her biological mother.

Of Drunken Showers

After the funeral, Mandla and I had a short holiday in the Eastern Cape, recapturing the magic we seemed to have lost in Johannesburg due to the hustle and bustle of our lives. At the end of the holidays, we picked up Hintsa, who was to start first grade, from Ma's farm and drove back to Johannesburg. On arrival, we found that Marita was back. She had a certain glow to her face and I could not resist asking, 'Did you meet someone in Soweto? You look very happy.'

She smiled before shyly answering, 'I didn't meet anyone. I reconciled with someone.'

I looked at her, then put on my confiding girlfriend tone. 'I didn't know you knew any guys from Soweto. So who is he? Where did you meet?'

This time when she answered her tone was defiant, 'It's not a "he". It's a "she".' O-ho! I didn't know she swung that way, but I took it in my stride and asked her how they met.

'Maria and I were in a cell together. We became partners in prison. I got out before her, and when she got out she didn't know where to find me. We bumped into each other again one day when I was in town and we started calling each other. I went to stay with her during the holiday because we both wanted to see whether it would work. Outside, I mean. She is so wonderful, MaHintsa! But now the problem is, I don't know how to tell MaRosie. She is my best friend but I don't want her to stop talking to me. She's a Christian, you know.'

Ha! My maid was having the eternal dilemma of the homosexual community: to tell or not to tell. I told her I was sure MaRosie would be surprised at first but would not stop being her friend. 'There are many homosexual people in Alex and I know she knows some of them. Besides, Jesus loves everyone, so she cannot say she is a Christian if she does not accept that you love and are giving love, whoever it is that you love.'

I, for one, was happy that she had found love. She was truly glowing with joy.

Mandla was back at work and back to being AWOL at home. This time his excuse was that he and his colleagues were allegedly busy planning their medical budget, including equipment purchases and repairs and, of course, pharmaceutical purchases.

This was their annual beginning of year arrangement, but for some unknown reason this year he seemed to be even more absent from home. When I asked him why this was, he went on the attack by telling me that since I expected him to pay a significant share of the bills, I should not whine about his hard work. I was taken aback because I genuinely missed him, but decided to look at the positive side – his absence from home meant there would be no drunken orgies with characters who expected me to wait on them hand and foot with platefuls of pap and gravy for their braai with meat poached from my refrigerator.

Lauren, who – like half of Joburg – often spent the holiday season in Durban with her children, was also back and setting up her class schedules for Wits commencement week. She told me about her holidays over the wall. It turned out that Zunaid also happened to be in Durban visiting his family. 'Being a lady, I do not kiss and tell, but I *can* tell you that some of the things that happened would have made HRH Queen Elizabeth blush. In fact, I think I can now safely compare my amorous excursions to those of Fergie.' I could just imagine it. Lauren as Fergie complete with Weight-Watchers. I laughed, but was feeling more than a little jealous. My husband was always working late, complained of being tired, and hadn't shagged me since our return from the holidays. 'So is it serious?'

Lauren laughed, with a glint in her eye, grabbed her phone and told me she was going to send him a saucy SMS because she was thinking of him. He immediately called her to make plans for the evening. With MaRosie now finishing work at five on the dot, I wondered who was going to look after the children. I didn't have to wonder long. 'Can you take the kids?' she turned to me, as an afterthought.

Feeling like an old spinster aunt, the married woman in me answered, 'Yeah sure. Why don't they come for a sleep-over? I can set up the tent and sleeping bags and they can camp out in the garden?'

This pleased Lauren. 'Darling. I absolutely adore you. You are the best friend ever.'

Like me, Siz had a few weeks off before the formal opening of her offices and she spent the time playing 'mommy-in-waiting'. It was a good four months to go before the baby would be with us, but Siz was going crazy with preparations.

It's amazing what the idea of motherhood does to transform a woman – even one who is not physically giving birth. She asked me to accompany her shopping, and we spent the days wallpapering the room she had decided to convert into a nursery for her upcoming non-biological baby. Siz would spend hours at the mall buying baby clothes and then bring her purchases to either Lauren or I to approve. 'Should we tell her that the child will probably outgrow his clothes before long?' I asked Lauren.

'We should be telling her to relax since it's a few months to go yet, but don't bother. I tried and she told me I was just jealous of her relationship and her upcoming child,' Lauren responded. I let it go. Siz was already making plans for shopping excursions to New York so she could go the designer route and buy the baby a full wardrobe from Baby Gap. She looked so happy and so in love, so I held my horses.

Would she come back around to being the crazy girl we knew and loved? New fathers who whine about being ignored probably felt like I did then. In addition to Siz's new baby, Lauren was getting sex and I wasn't. Shit.

As it was, Lauren reminded me that after a few weeks of changing nappies, burping and sleepless nights, she would be close to normal and would treat her child like the annoyance all babies were. Vuyo was just relieved that his wife was this accepting of his mistake and indulged all her baby plans.

Meanwhile, the arrival of a baby warranted a need for a domestic worker in Siz's household, but our friend was not going to make the same mistake twice. She asked Lauren if MaRosie's sister would come and assist with the baby. Lauren slapped her forehead for not having thought of it before and said that she would certainly ask MaRosie to ask her sister MaNeo. 'With the experience MaNeo has had with all her bastard grandchildren, it should be a breeze for her.' Then, tongue firmly in cheek, Lauren added, 'And since she stays in Alex,' winking at me, 'you do not need to worry that she will be the Camilla to your Diana, huh Siz?' Siz had forgiven Vuyo enough to be able to laugh at this one and I had to join her. Trust Lauren to find a royal family equivalent of the Vuyo-Pertunia-Siz saga.

While waiting to start work, I was running around shopping for the First-Grader-to-be, who was overly excited to be going to big school. 'Mommy, after I finish Grade One, how many years before I can become president?' Here I am enjoying the holidays and not too keen to get back to the office, and this itsy bitsy boy is thinking about his future job?

'Not long my darling. You will just finish primary school, then high school, a couple of university degrees, a few years of work, and then you can try to be president. Unless you are talking about being class president – that you may be able to do much sooner,' I teased, chucking him under the chin.

Two weeks after our return, Lauren and I decided to throw her a baby shower at my house. There were still more than three months to go before its arrival, but Lauren and I just needed an excuse for a party. Mandla, Hintsa and Lauren's kids went over to Siz's house to help decorate the baby's room – meaning the kids would be ordered to do some work and Mandla and Vuyo, in 'supervisory roles', would be downing some beers.

In order to avoid having to explain the various issues surrounding her baby, we made it a rather small and intimate gathering. Lizwe flew in for the shower and we brought in our other best friends – our maids who, fortunately for us, were equally avid party people. (Aside, of course, from the religious MaRosie – she was sticking to her orange juice, but her shebeen queen of a sister could drink Mandla and all his mates under the table.) Marita, in her tentative 'I'm-not-sure-what-you'll-say' voice asked whether she could invite her girlfriend Maria, whom she wanted to introduce to her very best friend MaRosie. I didn't know how MaRosie would take it, but I said yes. In truth, I also wanted to meet the woman who had made my Marita so happy.

On the day of the shower, Marita's girlfriend came early to help with the cooking. I don't know what I expected but she certainly was not it. Maria was slender, dark, beautiful and very feminine, and she was driving! Hoo! Marita had told me she was educated, and had had a good job before incarceration, but for some reason I expected some 'Just-arrived-from-Nongoma' type chick. Not this classy dame.

Marita came to the living room where we all were and said shyly, 'Everyone. This is my partner, Maria,' and then proceeded to introduce each one of us. MaRosie held on to her orange juice glass a little too tightly on being introduced. Lizwe, ever the diplomat, gave her a warm smile. Lauren, who I had not told, dropped her jaw so far it was in danger of being stepped on. MaNeo, MaRosie's sister who had accepted the job with Siz and had come for an introductory visit, did not seem to care as long as her glass was sufficiently supplied with gin and juice. And Siz, who always had a smart-ass remark to say about my maid, whispered what many in that room may have been thinking. 'Why didn't you tell me your maid swings that way?'

Of course I just asked her how any of that was her business.

Maria was quite handy and, after the initial shock to the rest of the attendees, she rolled her sleeves up and assisted us in getting everything ready. Maria made the salads and volunteered to do the 'guess-the-present' mixture for the future mother. To her credit, it tasted nasty. There was some of that so-called babies' 'fruit' food that, when any mother tastes it, swears never to give to their child, mixed with baby cereal and some tomato sauce. Yuck. I truly believe that pregnant women get constant heartburn because they are anticipating the crappy concoction that they may have to partake of at the baby shower if they fail to guess correctly what gifts are in the bag. Fortunately for Siz she was not actually pregnant, but she did gag when she was fed a spoonful after failing to guess that Lauren had wrapped up a baby monitor.

As is tradition, when the receiver guesses correctly, the giver has to consume the nasty stuff and I was the next person to gag after Siz correctly guessed that my gift was a car seat.

After a few drinks Siz turned to Maria and said, 'What's a beautiful girl like you doing being a lesbian?'

I was very embarrassed – in the way of every PC straight person who wants to know, but would never ask. Kind of like a white person who believes him- or herself to be liberal, asking a hip city-girl just exactly how they perform their tribal dance because he/she believes that all blacks are tribal. I am sure Maria had heard this type of ignoramus question before because she said, 'I think I knew I was not attracted to men from the get-go. Sure, I liked hanging with them and even tried the whole sex thing but I never felt anything with them, just felt dirty afterwards.'

Then Siz the Inquisitor turned to Marita, reminding her that she had been married before.

Marita laughed, '*Ag* Auntie Siz, if you were married to the man I was married to you would never want to be with a man ever again!' Then she looked lovingly at Maria, 'Nobody has ever made me as happy as Maria does,' and Lauren and I, ever the romantics went, 'Awwww.'

Lizwe, who was also by now half-drunk said, 'Siz, your problem is that you are not adventurous. I had a lesbian encounter when I was in college.' Siz was speechless and I must have had a pretty surprised expression when I asked, 'What? How come I never heard about this and I know all your little college secrets?'

'See, you don't know everything ...' grinned Lizwe slyly. It seemed one day Lizwe had gone to a strip club to support a friend who was a dancer. After a few too many shooters, they went to this stripper friend of hers' house and one thing led to another. Seeing the look on her sister's face though, Lizwe was quick to mention that there had not been a repetition of the lesbian action on her part.

Siz finally got her speech back. 'Oh my God. You are such a wild child. No wonder you spent so many years in college. You were too busy experimenting, hey li'l Sis!'

Not to be outdone, the freshly liberated Lauren had to add her bit. 'Well, actually Zunaid told me the other day – while we were doing some move from the Kama Sutra – that there is a bisexual in every one of us.'

MaRosie, who had been looking very uncomfortable throughout Lizwe's Lesbian story and, after ascertaining what bisexual meant, said, '*hayi, nix*, that cannot be true. Me, I don't want to touch a body that looks just like mine. And how can you have children? The Bible says you must marry and multiply.'

I don't know whether all the sex talk had made Marita and Maria all hot and bothered or whether the alcohol had freed up any remaining inhibitions, but the lovebirds were by now very busy with the public displays of affection. The tongue-locking that went on between the two of them would have made Madonna and Britney blush ... never mind MaRosie. She stood up, making some excuses about going to check on the children and scuttled out of the room. It certainly looked like the two lovers had forgotten there was anyone else there; they didn't even come up for breath. The silence and the throat-clearing from Lizwe finally snapped Maria and Marita out of it.

'*Ag* sorry hey,' slurred Marita, casting a drunken and not even slightly embarrassed eye around the room. 'Let's go to the cottage, come on baby.'

To say we were speechless at Marita's hanky-panky in the sitting room would be an understatement. We all just looked at each other and started laughing.

MaNeo rescued the party. Unfazed, as if this happened every day in her house, she continued the conversation where she had left off, saying loudly, 'If it's a boy, one thing you must always be careful of is to make sure you hold his weenie down when changing him, otherwise he will pee in your face.'

I, alas, could not come up with any interesting new baby anecdotes in my drunken stupor. The only advice I dolled out was on the wisdom of disposable nappies. '*Haa usile mhan MaHintsa. Nawe uyazi kuthi* a child cannot just wear those sweaty things. They need the cloths that are comfortable!' said MaRosie.

I was not going to argue with a veteran child-rearer, so I did the wise thing and shut up. Siz's upcoming motherhood had got me harbouring ideas of having a sister for Hintsa. After all, I didn't want him to be spoilt and I would like a mini-me. Then I recalled the weight gain, the sleepless nights, needless worries about little illnesses … I reassured myself that should I ever have maternal cravings, I would adopt. I mean, here I was still struggling with stretch marks six years later. Besides, wasn't the world already overpopulated? Rather look after children already here …

I fell asleep on the living room floor with a half-empty glass of chardonnay. What I do recall is that when I woke up, maids and madams – sans Marita and Maria – were strewn on the floor, and for that morning, our financial and social classes were forgotten and we were just women.

CHAPTER 19

Will I be your Valentine?

It was a much more sober Marita who spent the week after the baby shower dodging me out of sheer embarrassment. I decided to help her out of her misery and went to her room one day after work. 'So, Ms Marita. Are you avoiding me? I don't see you any more …'

She shuffled her feet, started removing some absent dust from her T-shirt. 'I am so sorry about what happened at the baby shower, I am soo soo sorry. I never drink wine and I was not remembering anything … I think it all went to my head. I am sorry.'

'There is nothing to be sorry about,' I answered wryly. 'In fact, I can hardly remember what happened myself. So, what are you girls planning for Valentine's Day?' I thought this line of questioning would signal that I had no hard feelings – plus it was a subject closer to my heart, although I would probably not be doing anything.

'Maria said since this was our first Valentine's Day out of prison and together, she wanted to make it special. She said that she would surprise me.' Marita answered, blushing. How charming. I could not remember the last time Mandla made me blush.

Mandla had been distant over the last couple of months. Sure, he had never been the overtly romantic type, but I wanted the man who was with me in East London, the man who was bringing me lunch at work when Ma was around. Now all I had was a husband I rarely saw and when I did, he was 'off to the surgery'.

Better turn my attention to the affairs of those around me. 'I forgot to ask, what does Maria do anyway?' I asked Marita.

'Oh. She is really a wonderful person, you know,' Marita gushed. 'She is an activist and works with girls who have been raped.'

Wow. I was impressed. Good-looking and worthy. 'So what was she in prison for?' Marita started laughing. 'What? Did I ask something funny?'

'Actually it's not funny. It's … well, it's sad-funny. Maria was raped. She told this man who was coming on to her that she was a lesbian and he attacked her in anger. It was horrible. She went and reported it, but the police kept saying they had too much to do. She knew the *ouk*, so I don't know why they just didn't arrest him – maybe because she also told the police she was a lesbian. Anyway, she decided to teach him a lesson herself. Ja. Invited him for drinks with some of her friends in Soweto. When he was good and drunk, they tied him up and beat him. She says he was crying *stukkend*, begging for mercy. But after that he went and reported them and she was arrested for assault.'

Poor Maria, I thought. No justice for her but justice for her rapist; our country definitely needed to look into changing the rules in favour of women. Marita shook her head at the injustice of it all. 'Imagine that. He raped her and the police do nothing because she likes women, but they arrest her because she has beaten a man. Why didn't they start laughing and say, "What type of man are you to be beaten up by women?" *Ag* man. It is so unfair.'

Meanwhile back at my ranch, my husband continued with his late nights and working weekends. I hoped Valentine's Day could recapture the magic, so as the day drew closer I tried to feel him out. 'Why don't I call your mother and ask her to look after Hintsa on Tuesday, then you and I can go for dinner, catch a movie afterwards and see what else we can get up to?' I suggested, with a saucy wink for good measure. Wasted effort, actually, since he was looking at the newspaper by the end of my statement. 'Hmm. Let's talk about it later babes.' Alrighty then.

When I revisited the topic again later that night in bed, he got very touchy.

'Look, Thandi,' (Thandi? Thandi? What happened to babes?) 'I am very busy at the surgery right now and would appreciate some support from you instead of this clingy, needy woman shit. We have bills to take care of and I have to work so that we can do that.'

I knew I had probably lost the Valentine's battle, but I didn't want to let it go. 'Babes, I miss spending time with you. We never do that any more. You are always out with Chukwu in Soweto when you aren't working and I am like, just a MOTHER and not even the woman you love any more. Besides, it's Valentine's Day on Tuesday,' I whined.

'Look, I don't know where you are going with this, but we have never celebrated Valentine's Day and I am not about to start now, seven years down the line. And I have absolutely no idea what you are talking about with our not spending time together. You know what I think? I think you have been talking to Siz and you are having a "Two can play that Game" moment. You should know by now that I am no Morris Chestnut, so let that Valentine's shit go. Now, I have work tomorrow and I am going to sleep.'

And, with a token kiss on the cheek after that long speech, Mandla turned his back on me.

'Damn him,' I thought as I turned my own back and tried to get to sleep without success. I thought about doing the old waterworks manipulation trick, but decided against it. Mandla hated tears and would jump to placate me but I thought I would rather save it for another moment. It didn't stop me from thinking it may have been better if my husband was Morris Chestnut, though!

When Valentine's Day came around, I was still sulking, but if Mandla noticed, he never let on and bade me goodbye like all was candy and roses. 'Effin bastard,' I muttered as he kissed me goodbye. 'What was that, hon?' he asked.

'I said "effin bastard" because today is Valentine's Day and I am just feeling a little blue and unloved.' Hey. It was never too late. But Mandla responded with a laugh. 'Let it go babes. I do not give a hoot about Valentine's Day and I am not about to go on a shopping spree for something I don't believe in.'

Well, obviously he was not going to jump, so I guess I would have to join the tired old cliché bandwagon of Valentine's Day being a 'capitalist conspiracy to squeeze money from the middle class' if anybody asked me about my plans. It didn't stop me getting bothered when I observed, as I drove to and from work, fellow women with arms full of roses, looking up to their men with adoration. Ahhh. I would go to the video shop and rent chick flicks tonight. *Bridget Jones' Diary*, *Waiting to Exhale* – and I was NOT making dinner when I got home. That decided, and having cheered myself up a bit, I got out of the door and who should I bump into but Marita's Maria, holding a bouquet fit for the Queen of England. Maybe this lesbian Soweto chick could teach my Mandla a thing or two about how to treat a woman. 'Hey, Happy Valentine's Day,' I forced a smile.

'Happy Valentine's to you too. Any plans for the evening?'

I thought about trying to shock her by saying, 'I am going to bring home a pizza and share it with my son, then watch chick flicks by myself while consuming a tub of ice cream because I know my husband does not care enough to be home on time. Then maybe I will masturbate myself to sleep.' But I decided against it as I realised there's proba-bly little that could shock Maria. 'My husband says it's a surprise,' I lied. I wonder why women always defend the men they love from other people? 'What do you have planned?'

'I'm taking Marita to Market Theatre to catch a play after work. Then afterwards we'll grab some dinner and see where the evening takes us.'

Flip. MY MAID IS BEING TAKEN OUT and here I am, The Madam, with nary a thing to do. Since Marita is no longer using her money for going out with MaRosie, has no children to support and is pampered by her compan-ion, I wondered: was I paying her too much? 'You sound like an envious old maid,' I told myself, 'get a grip, Thandi.'

My heart felt a further stab of pain on arrival at the office. My personal assistant, single and very much a 'looker', appeared to have charmed all her beaus into sending her flowers, and her office looked like a branch of Interflora. Upon seeing the flowers, I almost made a U-turn out of the office so I could go and buy myself flowers and pretend that Mandla had sent me something, but alas she had already seen me empty handed. She wished me Happy Valentine's day in the kind of smug and slightly patronising voice I imagine happy singletons always give the old-marrieds.

'Yeah yeah. Sweetie, don't let your personal stuff clutter the office. One bouquet on the desk is fine but more than that just looks tacky. Now, can we get on with the business of running Gauteng Tourism? I need you in my office to take notes.'

I am a bitch, I thought, as I looked at her putting her flowers behind her desk. But surely I am allowed to be a bitch once in a while? Still, I apologised for my tone, blamed it on a busy morning with Hintsa and then teased her about her bevy of admirers when she came to take notes of the day's priorities.

As if that were not enough, before leaving the office, Lauren called me to tell me she was going to dinner with Zunaid and asked whether I would mind checking in on her kids, 'since you don't believe in Valentine's Day anyway.'

'Sure girl,' I forced my umpteenth smile for the day. 'I was gonna grab a pizza for Hintsa – should I grab an extra one for them too?' I asked, a tad too sweetly. And then the bitch in me came out. Again. 'I certainly hope he doesn't take you to some vegetarian place where all they serve is the so-called "food" they offered us at the spa.'

'Actually, he is taking me to his brother's newly-opened restaurant in Winchester Hills. The steak there is apparently to die for and the dessert chef trained in France – he makes the most mouth-watering chocolate mousse ...' She paused. 'You sound a little bitter, hon. Another Valentine's Day that Mandla refuses to acknowledge?'

I was seething. 'Aw shuddup you, or I may rethink that whole offer of treating your kids!' I said with finality, hanging up the phone.

Lauren. My assistant. Marita. Oh why did I tie myself to marriage? Had I been so afraid of being lonely that I had chosen to get married to a less than perfect man? But then again, apart from my father, did the perfect man exist? Oh, I was doomed to a boring life of matrimony with a shade of romance on my birthday and on annual vacations. I wished I could burn down Hollywood for the misconceptions it had given me of marriages that have a 'happily ever after' and absolutely no dissatisfaction on either side.

I did not know why this romance stuff was bugging me so much this year. Since the average South African life expectancy is seventy, if one excluded death by HIV/Aids-related illnesses, and I was in my mid-thirties, was I technically having my mid-life crisis? I remember a friend of mine who had a seemingly splendid marriage, but got divorced from her husband after she had an online relationship with another man. I could now relate to the sense of dissatisfaction which had seemed fictional to me at the time. It was the dissatisfaction of being alone, even in the presence of him-whom-you-love because *he* is not communicating his love the way it should be communicated. The symptoms were all there – disillusioned with my textbook-perfect marriage as symbolised by my textbook-perfect husband, a propensity to want to grab the firm asses of twenty-something-year-old men and a sex drive that far surpassed that of my quite virile husband. Was Lizwe right after all? Were men only good in uncommitted relationships?

When I arrived home I was pleasantly surprised to find flowers on the dining room table. The unsigned card read: 'To my Favourite Girl, With Love'. Dare I hope that my dear sweet husband had had a change of heart? But the hope was short-lived as I got an SMS from my father: *Hey beautiful. Hope you like the flowers.* I SMSed him back, saying I hoped he liked the bottle of liqueur and the continental recipe book I had sent him. I should have called my father instead of doing the short message thing, but he knew me too well and I would end up whining about what Mandla was not doing. Given the fact that my father already thought Mandla was not good enough for his little girl, it was better for him not to hear it.

Sure, it was nice to get flowers, but getting them from my father was utterly duh. It's like being in high school without a date for the dance and your parents reassuring you that it was the guys' loss because you were very beautiful and a great conversationalist etcetera, and you knew for a fact that if your mother had bought you that padded push-up bra you wanted you would have had a date, ugly or not.

Meaningless, I tell you. The only other person I might have been able to whine to and examine my feelings with would have been Siz, but I knew she would be untouchable on this day. Vuyo, hoodrat or not, always knew how to impress women. Maybe that is why he had so many children from so many different ones, I thought sourly.

Marita was waiting for her date when I stomped into the kitchen. Damn she looked good; she was a vision of chic with her blonde hair framing her face and a red satin dress with a V-neck that brought out the best of face and cleavage. I was jealous, so instead of just complimenting her I asked, 'So how's Hintsa been today?'

On hearing my voice, my son came tearing down the corridor holding a cut-out Valentine's heart with 'I love my mommy' written in neat, large letters (in what I presume was his teacher's writing) and dabbled with multi-coloured paint splodges (that I know he had done). I treated that little cut-out heart like an expensive work of art. I hoped Hintsa had inherited the romantic genes from my side of the family and would one day make some woman happy on Valentine's Day.

'Thank you baby,' I said with tears in my eyes. Seeing

that Marita was about to launch into a tale of her upcoming romantic escapade, I excused myself with the lame 'I-need-to-use-the-bathroom' ruse. 'Have a nice evening with Maria,' I added dismissively.

I went to the bathroom where I looked at myself critically in the mirror. I wasn't a bad-looking woman. Sure, the ass could use a little toning, but there were many girls ten years younger who would kill for my flawless skin. And many more half my age who were not going to the matric dance because they didn't have my beautiful 'come hither' eyes or my full and inviting tits that looked like they could feed all of Africa and still look perky. So what was my husband's problem? Why was I about to eat pizza on Valentine's Day with a bunch of kids, while even MY MAID was being taken to dinner by her significant other?

'Babes,' I said to my son when I got out of the bathroom, 'why don't you go and call Junior and everyone next door and we can have a pizza party?'

'Yeah! Mommy, you are the coolest mommy in the world. I love you!' Amazingly, for a six year old, my son was still not ashamed to show affection to his mother.

When Mandla returned I saw him looking at the flowers on the table. 'From my dad,' I volunteered unasked. Damn, there was no signature. I should have made him believe that I had got them from some young, hot, virile stud. 'That's nice of him,' responded Mandla and proceeded to chat to me as if it was just another ordinary day.

I said nothing and acted as if everything was fine. Then I started to wonder about this funny characteristic that men have ... They fail to read your displeasure, then twenty years later, they tell you that they never knew you were unhappy because you didn't say anything. It seems the only non-verbal communication men seem to understand is the withholding of sex, and since most of us enjoy that as much (or more) than men, we rarely use that weapon unless the situation is really drastic.

Honestly, after being with someone for more than two months, a man should know the signs of displeasure when a woman answers his penetrating questions in monosyllables. I know I should not make gross generalisations about men, but you cannot believe how therapeutic generalisations are for a woman who feels scorned.

CHAPTER 20

Go Thandi, it's your Birthday?

After the annual Valentine's Day massacre of my heart, life returned to normal in my household. I decided against analysing my feelings with my girlfriends. I did not want them all up in my business and they would no doubt make a few none-too-subtle hints to Mandla. I was, after all, the strong one – or at least I wanted it to appear that way. I was the one everyone went to with their problems and doubts, the one who could handle her own issues. A tough, independent, self-reliant child of the struggle.

Besides, I knew from past experience that whining to my friends would not bring me closer to my husband. He would just complain about how I always air our dirty laundry to the world (never mind that 'the world' is my two best friends).

Hintsa was settling into his school routine nicely and my office walls, like those of any proud mother, were pasted with his artworks. Had my son been born a century and a half earlier he would have given Vincent Van Gogh some tough competition, but as it was, I was sure he was a reincarnation of Sekoto. With all my motherly bias, I was convinced that if my son decided not to run for the presidency, he would be the next big thing in the world of art.

On the first Saturday of March, the girls and I had our usual brunch and the heated debate of the day was the failure of what we had thought was a revolutionary Beijing conference to move women forward.

'I have to say that *we* have gone further than most women in the world, girls,' I put forward my case and a half-empty bottle of chardonnay. 'We have parents who did not force us into marriage to older men so they could get lobola, we have professions, families, and, in the case of you and I, Siz, we have men who are not that bad – and you, my dear Lauren, have the Kama Sutra man.'

'That is true,' said Lauren, sitting herself comfortably in the lotus position, looking as though she was ready to give a lecture, 'but the battle is not won yet. In spite of the civilised lives we all live as daughters, as wives, as sisters, as mothers, we are expected to serve first. Our needs still come second – or in your case, Thandi, third to those of your husband and child.'

'You are right, Lauren. And so, I would like to propose a toast,' said Siz, raising her glass drunkenly, 'to a world where women, who rule the world anyway, place all men underground and bring them up only to carry heavy loads or when we need sex. To Beijing and beyond.'

'Hear, hear,' Lauren and I said, raising our glasses.

'You know what bothers me, lasses?' I said.

'We don't but we are sure you are going to tell us,' replied Lauren, the smart-ass.

I ignored her. 'What bothers me is that in South Africa, although we are supposedly equal, it's the bloody men who are busy threatening us and shooting us and our kids when we break up with them.' (I will admit that when drunk, my philosophy sinks to the level of a *Daily Sun* reader.)

'Unless you are Siz,' Lauren added with a chuckle.

When Mandla came in later, having overheard our drunken revolutionary war cries, he knew better than to ask me to do anything in kitchen. Like the well-trained man he is, he went ahead and prepared supper. There were times when my husband just pissed me the hell off, but there were times, like this, when I just loved him to infinitesimal bits.

In late March it was time for the annual Feast of St Thandi, also known among pagans as my birthday. My birthday fell on a Friday but, dedicated worker that I am, I did not call in sick (it would have been a little obvious anyway). After school, Hintsa was going off for the weekend to visit his grandmother in Soweto. This had all been arranged because my significant other, whom I often underrated in the romance department, had apparently planned some wonderful surprise for me. With an air of mystery, he suggested that we ride to work together and he would pick me up at the end of the day.

'What are we doing? Tell me tell me ...' I squealed, excited as a child as we weaved through the morning traffic.

'You are just going to have to be patient, babes. You'll see later,' he grinned, and then kept me quiet by acting all preoccupied. I could play the game, although that certainly had me guessing. I also kept telling myself that if his surprise did not meet my romantic expectations, I would still holler and grin and act like it was the best present ever. All the effort he had put into whatever it was, had to count for something.

I was surprised alright. But not in the way I had hoped. An hour before he was supposed to pick me up, Mandla called. 'Babes. Can you ask your PA to drop you at home? I'm at my mother's – I came to drop Hintsa and my mother wants me to take her to Southgate to do some grocery shopping. I don't know when I will be done.'

Of all the lousy, messed up excuses! I could not believe that this bloody bastard whose heir had caused me so many hours of labour, was foregoing my birthday to be with his mother. My mother-in-law had always been quite supportive of me, but on this day she was not on my favourite person's list. That was the thing with my mother-in-law, though. No matter how great our relationship was, she was like the favourite wife in a polygamous marriage – whenever she wanted the man she had to have him and the other woman be damned.

And the cheek of her son to ask me to ask my PA to drop me off – so that my underling could laugh at my humiliation after a whole morning of trying to guess the wonderful surprise my husband had for me. Surely he jested!

'Okay,' I tried not to sound too disappointed, but he could read me.

'Don't worry, I will be home soon and I will make it up to you. Love you.' And he hung up.

There was no way I would let on to my PA that my husband had stood me up for his mother, so I asked her to drop me at Johannesburg Art Gallery. 'Mandla is meeting me there and he is already in town so I know with the traffic at this time I would have to wait for him forever.'

'Sure,' she said, 'I wonder what he has planned for you? A romantic weekend somewhere probably. You go girl!' My assistant was taking advantage of the fact that we were out of the office to be less professional with me. When she dropped me at JAG, I waited to make sure her car had turned the corner, then took a speedy walk to Noord taxi rank. I taxied my way home, scrunched between a mother with a snot-nosed toddler and a young man who obviously had not heard of deodorants, with the taxi driver having insisted on *'Sifuni muhlale four four'*. I was getting more furious by the minute. Mandla would definitely feel my wrath when he got back home that evening!

But Mandla didn't come back that night. As soon as I got home, I poured myself a glass of wine. Then another. By nine in the evening, I resigned myself to staying home and micro-waved a Woolies frozen dinner. I then proceeded to get drunk and curse Mandla as I did so. I switched off the telly (they were all living happily ever after anyhow, not like my life!) and the last thing I remember was singing 'I Will Survive' before falling asleep on the couch.

On Saturday Mandla was still not back, and my feelings were yo-yoing from intense anger to immense worry that he had not called. I kept imagining him lying in some morgue somewhere, unidentified by his next of kin. My pride, how-ever, was greater than my worry and I would not call any-one to check on him as that would make me look like a woman who had been abandoned. If he was not home by Monday, I told myself, then and only then would I call his office and his mother, try to trace his movements and file a missing person report.

I couldn't wait that long. I called my mother-in-law under the pretext of finding out how my son was.

'Oh, he is fine. He was with his father in the car earlier. Do you want to speak to Mandla?' she asked.

I said no.

So everything was 'fine'? Mandla was cruising the streets of Soweto. Was it another woman? I hated having such ideas about my husband, but I couldn't ask and risk sounding like a jealous, possessive housewife. I preferred to be the intellec-tual, professional, perfect wife that I was. But I would kill him if he had been with some ghetto hoodrat.

Mandla came home, drunk, with Hintsa late on Sunday afternoon. I wanted to slap him for driving around in that condition with Hintsa, but he was spoiling for a fight as the best form of defence for a wrong he knew he had committed. I decided I would not give him the satisfaction of hearing me say, 'Where the fuck have you been?' Let him try to figure me out.

My anger, which had been building up since I talked to his mother, was now cold and calculating. I was planning to avenge his actions in a way that would surprise him, and hit him hard. In addition to being mad about my missed birthday fun, I was also furious that I'd had to stay indoors and hide from my friends in an attempt to make it seem as if I was away somewhere. I had literally spent the whole weekend in my bedroom, vegging in front of the television with curtains drawn, so that even Marita, who was probably too tied up with her romantic escapades to bother about me anyway, would not spot me. It had less to do with my pride and more to do with my plan to exact revenge that I did not mention this incident to my comrades-in-arms. In the battle of the sexes, you had to come out on top before you could tell the tale.

'How was your weekend with granny, sweetie?' I asked my son, smiling as though all was normal with the world. 'It was lovely, mommy,' he said, bringing forth his hand, which had been hidden behind his back. 'Happy Late Birthday.' Late? Yeah, just how I felt about my relationship with Mandla. In an attempt to make me feel better the bastard was manipulating me by getting Hintsa to present me with a bouquet of flowers and a belated birthday card to a 'wonderful mother and wife'.

'Sorry babes, it was one thing after the other with my mother,' Mandla drunkenly apologised. I could hear from the tone of his voice that he was egging me to yell my disappointments at him, so I deliberately did not jump at the bait. Instead, I cooked and consumed my dinner with Mandla and my son as if everything was just fine.

I read Hintsa his bedtime story and tucked him in. 'I'm glad you and daddy had a good time at granny's house, sweets.'

'We had a good time but daddy wasn't there most of the time. He was at Auntie Norma's house down the street.' The little informer quickly put his hand to his mouth. 'Sorry mommy. That was a secret. Daddy said I shouldn't tell you. Why doesn't daddy want me to tell you? Auntie Norma was very nice.'

I gulped. 'Because Auntie Norma wanted to surprise me with a present tomorrow at the office, sweetie … and now you have gone and spoilt the surprise.' (AS IF!) 'How is she?' It was the last thing that I really wanted to know.

'Oh she is really cool, mommy,' he answered innocently.

I don't think that Mandla had ever guessed that his son would say anything, little knowing that motherhood surpassed any manly solidarity.

Norma was Mandla's ex from his Baragwanath days. Now she was a nursing sister at some clinic in Soweto but they had been together for two years before I came along. In fact, he hadn't seen her since … then the penny dropped. Could Norma have been that fat woman Mandla was talking to at the cinema? He had introduced her as Norma. She was FATTER than me and not even pretty! And the fact that his mother, who was supposed to be my ally, allowed this to go on … now she was really on my shitlist. So that explained all those visits to his mother and the constant 'going to Soweto' trips. Was he doing this with Chukwu and Kamau, since he always seemed to be drinking with them – or so he told me? Was Kamau also cheating on Njeri? Misery, you see, loves company.

Emerging from my son's room, I went straight to the bedroom and locked myself in. Before I had even finished scrolling down my cellphone address book to Njeri's number, I was in tears. Lying, cheating bastard! When she answered I was hysterical. 'Njers? It's Thandi,' I sobbed.

'Thandi, is that you? You sound like you've been crying, what's wrong?'

'Njers, can I come over? I know it's late but ...' I didn't know how to continue.

'Sure hon. Bring an overnight bag and we'll talk when you get here.'

I could not confide in my friends at this moment because we were too close, but Njeri was just the person I needed. Her husband was my husband's friend and colleague. Maybe he knew something. Mandla was in the kitchen cleaning up as I emerged with my overnight bag.

'Babes? Where are you off to?' he asked.

'Don't talk to me you adulterous bastard,' I said cutting my words off with the banging of the door.

As I got in the car I saw Mandla trying to follow, yelling half-heartedly for me to come back, but I just slammed the car door and drove, at breakneck speed, to Njeri and Kamau's house. Fortunately, no traffic cops were around because I was not in the mood for polite chit-chat and would have taken my fury out on any man I saw, uniformed or not.

When I arrived, Njeri was waiting for me at the gate. She walked me inside. Kamau was nowhere in sight and neither was their little girl.

'Come in my friend. Sit down. I made a fresh pot of tea. I will just pour you some.' I sat down and sipped on the hot, sweet tea.

'Why do you think people in the former colonies can't sit down and talk without a cup of tea?' I mused out loud.

Njeri smiled, 'Tea and sympathy – one of the better things the colonial masters left us with, I guess. Now, tell me what's wrong.'

I thought I had calmed down, but as I told Njeri what had happened I started to cry again. Njeri held me tight, then yelled for her husband.

Kamau came in, looking as though he had been on the brink of sleep.

'Did you know about Mandla and That Woman?' Njeri demanded. Kamau looked at me sheepishly. 'I heard him and Chukwu talking about it one day, hon.'

'And you didn't say anything? Wait. Have you been going around sleeping with other women as well?' The little woman was daring the tall, big man to answer in the affirmative.

'No, of course not, sweetie. I just thought it was none of my business,' he answered.

'None of your business? You invite Thandi for dinner at your house, you go and eat at her house and yet you think somehow the fact that her husband is sleeping with another woman is none of your business? You make me sick. Just leave.' Njeri thundered and her husband left meekly, probably glad to go back to bed and escape his wife's venom.

Njeri set me up in her spare bedroom and said I could stay there for as long as I wanted. I thanked her but declined staying longer than one night. As I lay in bed tossing and turning, I recalled my daddy's words when I broke up with my first boyfriend: nobody dies of a broken heart. I tried to reassure myself with these words, but it was not working. I kept analysing and re-analysing my marriage.

What was wrong with me? What had made my husband go to another woman? Had I put on too much weight during our marriage? Was I not wearing enough sexy lingerie in bed? Had I failed to be there for him when he needed me? Was I not a supportive, caring wife? Was I not a wonderful hostess to our guests, a great listener whenever he wanted to talk? Why, why, why ... I asked myself a zillion times without finding an answer.

I finally managed a fitful sleep and woke up in the late hours of the morning. Njeri and her family had already left for the day's business and she had left me a note. *If you need to come back, feel free. Don't let him or his mistress break your spirit. IT'S NOT YOUR FAULT.* It was as though she had been reading my mind as I tossed and turned through the night.

I went back to my house to pick up my computer. As I opened the door, there was Marita, on her knees, applying polish to the veranda. Although I was dressed for work, my eyes were puffy from the night's crying. I must have looked a sight because she immediately went into crisis mode. 'MaHintsa? Why aren't you at work? Where did you sleep? Are you sick? Is everything all right?' she asked. Evidently my son and his father had already left.

'I don't want to talk about it,' I answered, but her sympathy and my anger were just too much for me and I broke down and started crying again. My maid, the girl I had employed to antagonise my friend, on this day became my rock as she held me and I cried on her shoulder. After what must have seemed like hours to her but what was probably ten minutes, I calmed down enough to get up and go to the bathroom. 'Do you want me to call your office and tell them you are sick?' she asked.

'No,' I told her. 'But if you can call and tell them I will be late that would be nice. And Marita ...'

'Ja, MaHintsa?'

'I'd love a strong cup of coffee?'

'Ja, of course,' she responded, my only ally in this whole

mess even though she did not know what was wrong.

I finished my coffee and drove myself to work. I was not going to let that cheating bastard kill my spirit, as Njeri had advised me. From now on I would drown my sorrows in my work, I told myself. After all, my work would never cheat on me – save for getting fired, and I could not get fired if I was working twice as hard, could I?

While my assistant was out for lunch, I looked up through the open door that connected our offices and saw Mandla walking in as though nothing had happened. As if my office was a public toilet he could enter and exit without so much as a suspicious glance. He was carrying a food hamper, which he placed on my desk. 'Brought you lunch, babes.'

No apology, no apparent regret, as though all was candy and roses in the world.

I thanked him politely and handed the hamper back to him. 'I have already eaten, thank you,' I added very quietly, 'Why don't you take this to Norma and you and she can eat together, because as far as I am concerned, as of yesterday, I no longer have a husband.'

'But babes, I can explain ...' Mandla tried to interject.

'I don't want to talk to you right now. Maybe, just maybe, we will talk when I get home. Right now, I would really welcome it if you left.' My voice was deathly calm.

'But ...'

'Mandla, get out of this office right now before I call security. I will have you know, the way I am feeling right now, I would have no problems whatsoever with you spending the night in jail for trespassing,' I said, reaching for the phone.

Mandla might have been a philanderer and a fool who left steak at home for a hamburger of a nursing sister, but he knew I would have no problem making my threat reality. 'We'll talk at home,' he said as he walked out of my office, greeting my colleagues cheerfully. But he knew the line had been crossed.

I deliberately got home late, just in time to put my son to bed. 'What's wrong, mommy? Where were you, I didn't see you in the morning,' Hintsa asked as I tucked him in. The boy must have sensed something amiss, and probably felt the Cold War between his parents. Children always get caught up in the middle of these wars. 'I am just tired, my darling, I went to work extra early this morning. And mommy will be working late for the next few weeks so I may not be here to tuck you in,' I said as calmly as I could.

'But why, mommy?' asked the little man, pulling at my heartstrings and making me feel like a bad mother for allowing my marital problems to get in the way of being there for him.

'Because mommy has a lot of deadlines. Do you remember when you told me your teacher said you and your class had to finish writing your alphabet otherwise you couldn't go on break?'

'Yes.'

'Well, mommy's boss does not want mommy to go home unless she has finished her work everyday.'

'But I thought mommy was boss?' Such an astute boy. I should have found a better way to wiggle out of this one.

'Yes, but mommy is only the boss in Soweto but there is a big boss in Tshwane.'

'Is the big boss in Tshwane with the President, mommy?' asked the innocent, finding a common string between mommy's boss and the head of state.

'Yes baby, with the President,' I replied.

'When I grow up, I am going to come and help mommy so that she won't have to work so hard and she can come home on time, okay?'

'Okay. Thank you baby. I will wait for you to grow up so you can help mommy,' I said with tears in my eyes. I felt even more anger towards Mandla for putting me through this.

I sat with Hintsa until he fell asleep, thinking through my rage, 'Here is the only good thing to ever come from Mandla.'

When I came into the bedroom, Mandla was already there, pulling on his pyjama bottoms. He had the grace to look embarrassed and even a little guilty. I noted the irony of his covering his manhood in front of his wife when he had been busy letting it loose elsewhere during the weekend.

He sat on the bed. 'Babes …' he began.

I turned to him and cut to the chase. 'Look Mandla. You have crossed the line of my tolerance. Firstly, the only reason I have not gone to sleep in the spare room is because I want to maintain some semblance of normalcy for my son. I have not decided whether or not I want to remain married to your adulterous self, but you would do well to keep conversation with me to a minimum until I decide what I want to do. Secondly, I know we said we would talk at home, but I do not feel like hearing whatever story you may have concocted for standing me up on my birthday to be with your ex, so stay the fuck away from me and don't even think of touching me.'

When Lauren and Nosizwe called me asking how my romantic birthday dinner had transpired, I was vague. 'You don't want to know,' was all I could offer. I was not going to unload my domestic drama because I had not yet decided what to do. Either they were both too busy with their lives, or they thought I was preoccupied with something else because they did not pursue the subject.

The weekend after my birthday Lauren and Siz came over with their presents for me. I was dying to unburden myself on them, but I did not say a word. Again, lucky for me, they did not notice that I was unusually quiet. Siz was busy telling me of her plans for her child, and even brought a list of schools she planned to interview with a view to placing the unborn child on their waiting list, while Lauren was full of news about Zunaid and their latest escapade.

'I am feeling a little crowded right now. Zunaid has reached that horrible possessive stage,' Lauren said.

'Girl, I know exactly what you mean,' I said, trying to sound normal and to get into the spirit of things. 'I had that with one of the guys I shagged in college. Siz, remember Stu?'

'Girl, don't I remember? Tall and toned and – as you loved to say – he had a package that defied the idea that men who work out shrink.'

'That's the one. Lauren, would you believe that man could lift my big ass in the shower? Anyway, we'd agreed to just "kick it", but he reached that weird stage where he wanted to possess me and to tell my friends and the whole world about him because he could not understand why I had not fallen madly in love with him.'

Siz had to put her tuppence in. 'Lauren, this dude was calling *me,* all, "What's wrong with your friend? I even told my mother about her, but she keeps blowing me off!" As though telling his mother was what she had been waiting for before falling madly in love with him.'

I laughed. 'Yeah. It works when you are looking for commitment by acting coy, but it can be truly nauseating when you just want something light. It's so transparently all about their fragile male ego – they are trying to ensure that they are the only man in your life.'

Lauren brought us back to Kama Sutra Man. 'But listen to this, you know Zunaid is one of those BEE Indian guys and now he is even asking me whether the reason I do not want to introduce him to my friends and family is because he is black.'

'So?' said Siz cheekily, 'Did you tell him that some of your best friends are black?'

'Did I ever! And he wasn't amused and I don't know what the big deal with him is. He has met my children and he has met you guys and that's the only friends and family that count,' Lauren responded.

'Girl. Your Zunaid has serious issues. Men leave women who demand commitment, because it makes them feel tied down. And here's a woman who is willing to give it up without asking for anything in return, cash or kind … Talk about role reversal!'

For the next three weeks, my house was frosty. In all that time, Mandla was coming home early and spending the weekends at home in a lame attempt to show me he was sorry. We were sleeping in the same bed, staying in the same house, using the same bathroom, but absolutely no words were exchanged. The worst thing about this was that, save for the tears I had shown Marita, I could not even share this with my friends. Serves me right for deriding the whole Vuyo/Pertunia saga to Lauren. How would it look if I stayed with Mandla after giving Siz such a hard time about it? I guess, feminist or not, a woman could never understand the actions of another woman until they had walked a mile in that other woman's Mahnolos.

I communicated with Mandla only when necessary and pretended all was well when Hintsa was around. I finally broke one evening during yet another funny Polka advert.

Having laughed out loud, it would have seemed petty to go back to the silence, so I decided to have it out with Mandla and ask the question that had been running through my mind since I found out about his infidelity: 'WHY?'

When he answered, I wanted to slap him. 'Look. I am really sorry Thandi. What happened was, I bumped into Norma that time at the movies,' (just as I thought, I said to myself), 'and she invited me to her son's birthday. At first it was all innocent, but she seemed genuinely interested in my life and you have been so busy at work …'

'So this is my fault now is it? I will have you know, it was you who went and slept with someone else. You, who flaunted your mistress to my son.' I was getting hysterical. 'You, who made plans for my birthday and ended up shacked up with some other woman. You, who acted like a dog. And you want to say it's my fault. Un-fuckin-believable!'

'Of course it was not your fault. And it's not her I want. You are the woman I married because I want to spend the rest of my life with you. I swear, I will never do that again and I promise to spend my whole life making it up to you …' he went on.

'And the fact that you married me and not her is supposed to make me feel better is it? How about the fact that you slept with her when you should have been sleeping with me? How about that?' By now I was yelling and crying.

My son walked in and held on to my dress. 'Who did daddy sleep with when he should have been sleeping with you mommy?' Oops. My voice was obviously octaves higher than I had hoped. I felt like a heel for having my child hear all this.

Later that night, with Hintsa asleep and me having calmed down a little, Mandla attempted another pathetic explanation. 'Look baby, I was selfish. I was stupid. It's just that, I can't quite explain it, maybe the best thing I can say is that I was feeling suffocated.'

'Suffocated? Was I the one who proposed? Was I the one who claimed undying devotion? Was I the one who claimed I could not live without me and duly paid lobola?' I had to let it go. There was absolutely no way he could explain this one.

There and then I decided 'two could play this game'. Sure, two wrongs do not make a right, but I felt I would only feel vindicated if I hit back. I smiled indulgently and told him it was all right, we could work it out. The trust was seriously eroded, but I had to spring my revenge on him as a surprise. Inside, though, I was seething. Space? Humph. I would show him space.

Although our lives had resumed normality on the outside, Mandla knew well it would be a long time before the trust could be rebuilt, particularly when I asked for a full STD test before I would even think of resuming bedroom relations. (At least he had had safe sex. So he said. But I certainly wasn't going to sleep with him sans raincoat – and condoms do burst y'know.)

The next two months passed by with my acting like all was normal and even going through the motions of enjoying sex, but the truth is that I do not know of any woman who enjoys sex when they have an underlying issue. Although most men believe the myth that sex has a healing effect and believe in the kiss-and-make-up theory – I blame Marvin Gaye and his 'Sexual Healing' hit.

I quietly plotted my revenge, arranging my ticket and accommodation for the time when I too would have 'my space'. On the third Friday of May, I drove to work as usual and stayed there until lunch time, after which I told my assistant that I was taking the rest of the day off. I also informed her to take any messages from anyone who called me and to tell them that I would only be able to get back to them next week. I then made tracks to my house to pick up a few items of clothing en route to Johannesburg International Airport, where I would be taking my flight out to Victoria Falls.

CHAPTER 21

A Dish Best Served Cold

On arrival at the landing strip that serves as an airport in Victoria Falls – or should I say, *Mosi oa Tunya*, which is what it was called before David Livingstone 'discovered' it – I took a shuttle to my chosen place of escape, the luxurious Elephant Hills Hotel.

'Welcome to Elephant Hills, madam,' said the concierge, ushering me into this castle where the only requirement for me to be queen was a credit card. 'Yes indeed,' I thought to myself, 'this is going to be Thandi's weekend.'

I had arranged for a spa visit and massage an hour after arrival so, after settling into my suite I switched off my cellular phone – international roaming or not, this was going to be quality me-time – slipped into one of the extremely comfortable hotel robes and made my way down to the spa.

The spa visit eased away most of the tension I had carried with me for the last few months. And I knew that after this weekend, I would be ready to let go of my anger, forgive and move on with my life and marriage. Because I would have exacted my revenge and, hopefully, taught Mandla a lesson in the process.

There are few things I enjoy as much as a coldly plotted

revenge when the party to be avenged does not suspect it. Methinks I would have made a great politician, or a great Hannibal-style military tactician. After all, revenge is a form of retaliation, so doesn't that make it part of 'all that's fair in love and war'?

I had not felt this free for a long time. I took an hour's nap, then took a ride into the centre of the small town, admiring the curios, trying on interestingly-woven hats and buying crocheted tops and dresses I knew I would probably never wear. I went to the Victoria Falls Hotel and played on the slot machines – an outing of sorts, I guess, since there were gambling facilities at my own hotel.

On returning to the Elephant Hills, I sat down in one of their exclusive restaurants and had a solitary, but not lonely, dinner. I was in the mood for letting it all hang out, so after dinner I went to the bar and ordered one of those cocktails with umbrellas in them that look nice on the menu and taste even better … as long as you don't ask what's in them.

A few minutes later a tall, dark god came and parked himself on the stool next to mine at the bar. He stood at over six feet, chocolate-dark and smooth shaven, save for the well-shaped goatee and sideburns that looked as though they had been measured with a ruler to ensure exactness. I could use a night with a man like him, I thought to myself.

I was stealing glances at him and having a few fantasies when he looked up and our eyes locked. The man had the most expressive eyes I have ever seen, and what his eyes were expressing now was naked lust. The godly illusion shattered and I knew I was lusting after a married man when, on opening his mouth, he said in a rich American drawl that unmistakably emanated from one of the Southern states, 'So. Where is your man at?'

Oh no. That pathetic pick-up line was far from Georgia

peachy. Of all the things to say to a woman – I knew there and then that he had not been on the dating scene in ages. But for this weekend, it was just me against the world and I was not going to let some meaningless thing like a wife or husband somewhere on Earth take away my sense of independence and enjoyment. After all, Siz and I had a rule in college that one was considered single as long as you were in a different postal code from your significant other. For this one weekend, I planned on being available.

When I heard his name I knew I was right about his background. He was from one of the bourgeois black families in the American South with long-time Spellman and Morehouse education. He even had a name to prove it, with numbers at the end, *nogal*. 'I'm Martin Lee Robert the Fourth.' At least it was not one of those unpronounceable black American names that just seem to be a haphazard combination of letters meaning little or nothing but that, when you ask the owner, apparently are AFRICAN. 'And what might your name be, beautiful lady?'

'My name is Thandi, Mr Martin Lee Robert the Fourth. Welcome to Africa. Are you enjoying yourself in the Motherland?' I flirted.

'But of course. There is so much good stuff to see.' He was so undressing me with his eyes. At least he knew a good thing when he saw it. 'So, you didn't answer me, where is your man at?' he continued.

'My husband is at home looking after our son. Where is your woman at?'

He smiled. 'My wife is at home looking after the house and our dog since we have no children.'

'And what are you doing here without her?' I asked, my curiosity piqued.

'I am actually here for work,' he answered, not elaborating.

But I wasn't letting go that easily. 'And what kind of work would that be? Are you a professional gambler?'

He laughed and explained that he was a senior lecturer of African-American History at the University of Chicago and I made a mental note: 'one of the twenty per cent or so of black American men who escaped prison and made a success of their lives'. I questioned him on it and he told me I watched too much television.

'Not at all. In fact, if I watched too much television, I would be assuming that you have five babymamas in five towns of one state and a male partner in the neighbouring state – if Ricki Lake is to be believed.'

He guffawed. The man had a sexy, wholesome laugh that I love in people. That laughter that starts from the stomach, lights up the eyes before rumbling in the throat and bursting forth like thunder ... a soul laugh.

'Actually I am quite familiar with your country,' I informed him.

'Really?'

'Yes, but why do you seem so surprised?' I asked.

'Because I have heard it said that you South Africans are like Americans. You think everyone wants to be South African and as such, you never travel out of your country. Besides, all the Africans I have met who have stayed in the States usually speak with an affected American accent and you have a distinctly African accent.'

I laughed. 'Actually I have done my own share of international sightseeing, but thank you for what I will presume is a compliment, although I am not quite sure what exactly an African accent sounds like.'

He was equally quick. 'That's easy enough – an African accent sounds like yours.'

I told him that I was, in fact, proudly African, hence the

maintenance of the accent in spite of six years of Yankee cultural domination. When he was not trying to pull the lame come-on lines, Martin was a strangely fascinating man and not just because he was the embodiment of a black Apollo either. He was a witty and intelligent conversationalist and time flew as we sat talking.

I found out that he was at Elephant Hills chairing a meeting with a number of other lecturers from other Midwest universities in similar faculties. The topic of discussion: 'African loss of identity in post-colonial Africa'.

'Do you have any African intellectuals here at the conference?' I asked, curious.

'No, we don't,' he answered.

'Excuse my boldness, but don't you think it's a bit presumptuous, and even patronising, for you folks to be discussing Africa without the presence of Africans?' I said, a bit perturbed.

'You are absolutely right, this seminar was planned haphazardly. But what say you come to our session tomorrow?' he invited.

I graciously agreed. As our discussion entered more personal territory, I found that Martin had one redeeming quality in his whole *bourgeois* persona (apart from his looks and his penchant for great conversation); he was a self-made man, which was rather surprising for a person who grew up in a comfortable environment.

'I refused to attend Morehouse, and instead attended UH Manoa on a basketball scholarship.'

'You were at UH, oh my ... when were you there?' What were the chances of finding a kindred spirit in a deep, dark African safari town?

'I was there from '96 to 2000, do you know anyone there?' he asked.

'Know anyone? Dude, I was there at the same time. You played with Carter?' And the conversation went on from there and time flew. I had forgotten the thrill of the chase and it was fun to let my hair down.

My relationships with the opposite sex had, since Mandla and I got married, been relegated to males as colleagues of self or partner, partners of my female friends, or family friends. The only male I had had any meaningful relationship with in the past six years, apart from my father, was Mandla and that, at the moment, wasn't exactly a no-holds barred situation. It was weighed down with the responsibilities of our son having a cold, my father visiting, Mandla's mother needing grocery money – the kind of relationship where one has to make such serious attempts at spontaneity, there is nothing spontaneous at all. And certainly nothing as relaxed and laid-back as the time I had just shared with Martin.

What happened next should not, in ordinary circumstances, have happened, but these weren't ordinary circumstances and I felt good knowing that I was giving the middle finger to my husband. The alcohol, and the presence of an attractive and, even more importantly, intelligent male was a gift from the goddess of revenge. I found it very liberating.

Martin and I cannot claim to have made love that night, it was something more primal, an animal need to connect after finding a kindred soul – if only for one weekend. It was passionate, beautiful, guiltless sex. We both agreed that our actions would not be repeated, neither in word nor deed, after this weekend as we were both attached. It would have been difficult to replicate them anyway as we lived continents apart.

After hours of passion, we took a catnap and then were

up at the break of dawn to see a sunrise over the falls. I would have liked to take some photographs with my camera phone, but I did not want to risk putting my phone on and running into a call from Mandla. Or anyone else for that matter. I also did not want to run the risk of being tempted to take a photo of this fellow I was having an illicit weekend affair with and thereafter forgetting to erase it. I could just imagine the questions from my son if he came across it while playing games on my phone.

'Let's go bungee jumping today!' I challenged Martin, after taking in the sunrise.

Bungee jumping seemed appropriate, somehow – I mean, this had been the first time I had slept with someone other than Mandla in seven years. Although I do not think 'sleep' is an apt word for the night we had spent together.

After throwing ourselves into the great void, we went back to the hotel and had a sweaty workout before showering and eating a satisfying brunch.

I attended the seminar session in the afternoon – admittedly, I didn't take in much of what was being said, I was so busy admiring my man of the moment and fantasising about what we would get up to that evening.

After another passionate night and a long, late morning in between, I bade Martin farewell. No email addresses or phone numbers were exchanged – we wanted to avoid complications.

CHAPTER 22

Of Love and Marriage

The flight was very eventful – but only in my mind, as I was actively reliving the occurrences of the weekend. I also kept a monologue going with myself on how I would respond to Mandla's anger when he questioned my disappearing without notice.

As I drove from the airport with Chiwoniso Maraire's 'Rebel Woman' blasting from my system, I felt every inch that ... and I felt oddly liberated in my rebellion.

I arrived at work on time and got on with the business of slaving for the government, but today nothing could get me down. When my assistant arrived, she came directly to my office and hugged me as if I was an eleventh century Catholic knight returned from the crusades.

'What the hell is wrong with you?' I enquired, bemused.

'Am I glad to see you,' she answered. 'Your man has been calling me ad nauseum, asking me what your plans were, wondering whether you had been hijacked in Soweto ...'

I laughed.

'What is so funny, Sis Thandi?' she asked.

'What's funny is that my husband was born and grew up in Soweto – now suddenly he lives in suburbia he starts thinking Soweto is not safe. If that isn't totally moving-on-up-to-the-eastside of him, I dunno what is.' I laughed again.

She lifted a brow and said, 'I don't mean to be all up in your business Sis T, but did you and Mandla have a fight?'

I responded, 'You are right, it's none of your business. Now, can we get on with work for the day?'

She got the message, but was still giving me a look. 'What?' I said.

'Nothing, just … If I may say, you look more relaxed than I have seen you look in months. And that suit looks really nice on you.'

'What, this old thing?' I smiled. 'I do look good, don't I? Thanks.'

I got on with the business of the day starting, as usual, with checking for any urgent correspondence. What do you know, twelve – count 'em – twelve emails sent from my home email address by Mandla. I looked at the last one. It read: *Thandi please if you see this email call home. Your phone is off. Your girls don't know where you are, not even Lizwe or Njeri. I can't find you, I don't know what to tell the boy.*

So like Mandla, always using the boy to make a point, taking advantage of my maternal instincts. How did I respond to this? I just pressed 'Delete' for all of them. I did, however, call home immediately to reassure Hintsa that I was okay. The little man had already gone to school, but Marita would give him the message when he got home.

While I was still checking my messages, my office door opened and, before my assistant could announce my guest, he strutted in like he was master of all he surveyed. Very commanding. Very sexy. I still didn't trust the bastard.

Mandla waited just long enough for the door to close before assaulting me with a barrage of questions. Firstly, though, I saw relief written on his face and I swear I have never loved him more than I did at that moment. The relief was quickly replaced by anger, to which I responded with unnerving calm. I think this unsettled him even more.

'Where have you been?' he stammered.

'Victoria Falls.'

'What the hell were you doing in Victoria Falls?'

'Are you checking up on me now?' I allowed a devious smile to play on my lips. 'I needed my space.'

I saw Mandla's mind ticking. He was getting it. Oh … So this was revenge? This dish had been served so cold that it had not immediately registered. I gave myself many cool points because it had made much more of an impact now than if I had avenged him immediately after his transgression.

'Why didn't you call, if not me, at least one of your friends to let them know your plans?' he asked, calming down.

Duh. The point was for him to worry and be angry, just as I had worried and been angry – an attempt at teaching him to understand his woman's feelings through empathy. And, hopefully, it would also ensure there would be no repeat performance. I knew, though, that he would never assume in a million years what I had been up to. My husband was bewilderingly overconfident about how great he is and how much I love him. Still, I had won this round; he had called my friends and my personal assistant, whereas when he had done his disappearing act, I had not called a soul.

He changed tactics. 'You know Marita is off during the weekends, who did you think would take care of our son and cook for him?'

Again, thin ice. I pictured it: my husband was the Titanic and I was an iceberg. I was so close to sinking him.

'His father does not work during the weekend, is not disabled, and is a highly able cook,' I shot back.

'Who were you with?'

Did he suspect something? 'I told you I needed space, this means I was by myself, what do you think?' I answered, looking him straight in the eye. And, of course the *coup de grace:* offence as the best form of defence. 'Did I ask you who you spent time with when you up and left me on my birthday for the whole weekend?' My voice was deathly calm. 'Would I have known if it weren't for my son? Was I the one who cheated on my spouse? How dare you? You know what your problem is, Mandla? Your problem is that you think you own me. With all due respect, your lobola fee was not that much and if you do not stop treating me like your personal property, I know my father will have no problem returning your lobola – maybe you can get some rural girl who will put up with your shit, or you could go to your Norma.'

'Why do you always have to bring up old shit, Thandi? I said I was sorry for all that, didn't I? Can't you just let it go?'

'Old shit to who Mandla? And why do you think that saying sorry makes everything candy and roses? You know what … you just don't get it. Eight years together and you don't get it Mandla. Maybe we shouldn't be together.'

He had been pacing up and down in my corner office like a caged animal, but these words stopped him in his tracks. He started placating me. 'You are right baby, I don't get it, but babes … I was just worried. I know now that you did this because you were angry about your birthday. I know sometimes I disappoint you when I don't prioritise our relationship. I'm sorry. Look, why don't we both bury the hatchet and try to treat each other better?' I must have looked pretty sceptical because he quickly added, 'To show you how serious I am about trying harder, how about lunch at Kwa-Thabeng today, and we can talk further if you need to talk?'

'No. I don't think that would be a good idea,' I answered icily. 'Let's meet at home and we can talk because, babes, we really need to talk.'

I saw the look of surrender that came over his face. It was the same look that the biblical Adam probably had when Eve said 'We need to talk' … right after he had laid the blame on her doorstep for giving him the Forbidden Fruit.

'Fine,' he said, shoulders slumped as he walked out. He knew it was not going to be pretty.

I got an SMS from my father not long after Mandla's departure: *Word has it you disappeared this weekend. What the hell are you up to?*

I responded quickly: *Who told you that?*

The double beep told me he had responded back: *Child. I am a trained journo. I never reveal my sources. Will call you now.*

He called and without any preamble, got straight to the point. 'So, are you going to tell your old man what you were up to?'

I told him I had gone to Victoria Falls. 'Mandla and I had a fallout and I needed space and time to think,' I said. Although what I had gotten up to was far from thinking.

'So tell me, are you finally going to divorce that pompous ass doctor?' he said, laughing.

'Daddy! Mandla and I are not getting divorced, but we are getting a separation because I need to think,' I said, and for the first time I actually vocalised what it was I was planning to do.

Then my father went on a rage asking what that bastard had done to me and threatening to come up to Johannesburg and put a bullet in his nether regions. I calmed him down, telling him that we were just growing apart. I loved Mandla, so it would not do to tell my father that he had cheated on me. Let him think I was the one who was being weird about our relationship.

Now that I knew what I was planning to do, I realised that

it would irrevocably change the lives of those nearest and dearest to me. I went through the day like a zombie, constantly asking myself where it had all gone wrong. It had seemed so perfect.

After work, I was happy to get home and see Marita and my son. He was equally happy, telling me how much he had missed me and how he and daddy had missed me at the movies. Although I had not missed the rugrat with all the activity I had going on during my weekend, I cherished the fact that he had missed me. In a few years he would be an adolescent and would not be able to wait for me to go on business trips so he could sneak girls (or, heaven forbid, boys) into the house. 'Where were you?' he demanded.

'I went to Victoria Falls for a meeting,' I lied. Then I lied again, 'I think your daddy must have forgotten because I told him last week.' Of course, I did feel a little bad about using the other parent to defend myself.

'So, what did you bring me?' he asked.

'Check in my bag. I have some stuff for you and Aunt Lo's kids. Can you take the cars to them?'

I had brought him and Lauren's children those wire motor cars that every child, except the suburb-raised kids, knows how to make, and that entrepreneurs sell at Victoria Falls at killer prices for the naïve tourists. I was soon forgotten as he ran next door to drop off the cars and play in the driveway.

A few minutes later the matron from next door walked into my home, grinning happily at me as though Princess Diana had come back from the grave. 'And just where have you been?' Lauren enquired, squashing me in a huge hug. She told me Mandla had driven both her and Siz nuts calling and trying to locate me.

'Girl, I will tell you all in good time, but first, how is

Zunaid?' I wanted to deflect attention and I knew there was nothing Lauren loved more than talking about Zunaid.

'Same ol', same ol'. Although, I've just put a new word into my Wits English dictionary based on Zunaid and his tricks,' she answered with a lascivious wink.

'Tell tell. You know I am always anxious for knowledge,' I laughed.

'Ready? The word is Yosexcise – meaning sexual exercising through yoga.'

'Right on, sensei.' Then I got serious. 'Look, could you keep Hintsa at your house for a while? Mandla is coming in any time and him and I … we need to talk.'

Lauren looked concerned. 'Is everything alright?'

Then it happened. I burst into tears and told her everything. Mandla's infidelity, my Victoria Falls escapade. I sat on the couch in my living room with her holding me and telling me that it would be alright. So much for me being the strong one. Here was Lauren stroking my Afro like I was one of her children, and me soaking her blouse with the waterworks. 'I thought I would feel much better after my little holiday affair, and I did up until now … but Lauren, how could I stoop to his level? I can't be with him any more.'

Lauren was hushing me and saying something about how I should not do anything rash when Mandla walked in. Knowing I needed some one-on-one time with my husband, she stood up to go. 'I'll be next door if you need anything,' she called, responding to Mandla's greeting with a withering stare. Seeing this, Mandla knew he was in trouble. He just threw down his briefcase before sitting on the couch opposite me.

'Okay, let's talk.'

And I let it out. I told him how I had felt betrayed. How he had broken the trust.

.I told him how I had gone to Victoria Falls in search of revenge and had found it.

That got his attention and his look of humility suddenly turned to anger. 'Y-y-y-you what?'

'I thought I would feel better about your cheating if I did the same thing. I don't. I can't trust you Mandla and I think we should separate for a while to figure out whether we want the same things from this relationship …'

Mandla didn't let me finish, 'You went and did the same thing that you accused me of doing and now …'

'Look. I know now that two wrongs don't make a right. But it's done. I can't be with you any more, Mandla. Now, either I can go and stay in a hotel with Hintsa, or you can go, but I am not staying under the same roof as the man who betrayed me and our marriage a day longer,' I said with a steely determination in my voice.

'Fine,' he yelled, and then more softly, 'Fine. I will go and you take as long as you need to think. I will come and pick Hintsa up for the weekends if that's okay with you.' He walked to the bedroom to pack his bags.

I waited for some feeling of victory, some sense of jubilation, but it didn't come. Was I doing the right thing?

I called Lauren and asked her to tell Hintsa to come home. Just before Mandla walked out we both sat down with the boy. We may have felt a wave of different emotions towards each other, but we both knew we loved our son and we must protect him from the pain we were about to cause him. 'Listen little man,' Mandla said with tears in his eyes, pulling him close and placing him on his knee. 'Daddy and mommy are having a few difficulties right now and daddy is going to stay with Uncle Chukwu for a while. You will be the man of the house while I am not here and look after mommy, won't you?' Trust Mandla to go and camp with his partner in crime, but I wasn't in a position to tell him who he could or could not stay with. After all, I was responsible for his impending departure.

The boy nodded on a sob and looking at me accusingly. 'Are you and daddy getting a divorce?' he asked.

Damn. Maybe this separation thing wasn't a good idea after all. Maybe I should have bitten the bullet and had Mandla staying in the house while trying to rebuild the trust. 'No baby, no,' I said, getting up and hugging him where he sat on Mandla's lap. Mandla put his arms around me in what became a group hug and what, for me, was the first moment of true sincere intimacy with my husband in a long time. The irony was that it was coming now, just as he was leaving.

We all cried quietly until Mandla abruptly broke the contact with me, lifted Hintsa off his lap and, rubbing the boy's head, said gruffly, 'See you on Saturday morning and we can do some fun things, eh boy?'

The boy responded by hanging on to his father's leg and it took some doing from both parents to disengage him.

Then Mandla walked out, suitcase in hand, into the darkness.

Epilogue

I love my life. I love my six-year-old Hintsa. I cannot do without my dependable, solid white maid Marita. I need my crazy friends Siz and Lauren to keep me grounded. And I miss the love of my life and the man I am separated from, Mandla.

As I sit here typing, I am waiting for the girls to arrive for a morning of decadence – I have made a chocolate mousse to go with the bubbly.

My son, a true child of the twenty-first century, has taken Mandla and my separation in his stride – it turns out most of his classmates live in single parent homes, so he doesn't feel different from them.

When Mandla left, he went to stay with Chukwu, then took out a six-month lease on a two-bedroom apartment. As things stand, he has only a month more on the lease, so I take this as a message that maybe he will come around and want to work something out.

Our once tense relationship is now comfortable. He comes to pick up Hintsa on Fridays for the weekend and picks him up daily from school to drop him off here. Yesterday when he came to pick up Hintsa he looked at me like a man looking at a woman.

'You look good babes,' he said. He had not called me that since he left.

'Thanks, you don't look too bad either. Cut down on the beer?' I said, noticing the receding stomach.

He laughed, then turned serious. 'I have something I want to say.'

'Sure, what's up?'

'Thandi. You are a good woman and you were a really good wife and mother. When I left, I was angry because of what you did in Victoria Falls, but I have thought about it and I know it was hypocritical of me. I am not saying what you did was right, but I messed up first and that was unforgivable.'

I was taken aback. That was the last thing I had expected him to say.

'And Mandla,' I answered, 'I am sorry that I realised too late that two wrongs don't make a right.' Then, being Thandi-who-never-wants-to-miss-an-opportunity, I asked, 'Is it too late?'

He did not answer but smiled at me as he walked out of the house with Hintsa.

I live in hope.

FINIS

Glossary

BAIE DANKIE: (Afrikaans) many thanks, thanks a lot
BARA: short for Baragwanath Hospital
BHUTI: brother

CAJONES: slang for 'balls', or courage
COSATU: Congress of South African Trade Unions – the amalgamation
   of South Africa's labour bodies

EISH: general exclamation to indicate surprise, sympathy or irritation
EISH MNTANAMI: eish, my child
EKASI: (tsotsitaal) neighborhood

HAA USILE MHAN MAHINTSA. NAWE UYAZI KUTHI: don't be silly
   MaHintsa. Even you know …
HAIBO: no (an exclamation that, when stated in isiXhosa,
   indicates surprise)
HAWU: hey
HAWU, SIS PERTUNIA. UYAZI KUTHI USIZ UYADLALA NAWE:
   y'know Siz is joking/teasing you …
HAYI NIX: nada, nope
HLONIPHA: respect

IBABALASI KUPHELA: only a hangover

JA NDIYAZI: yes, I know
JISSUS: (Afrikaans slang) Jesus

KA'AWA: traditional Hawaiian drink (also known in other Polynesian
   Islands as kava, ava etc.)
KANAKA MAOLIS: Native Hawaiians and first human inhabitants of the
   Hawaiian isles (they are to Hawaii what the Aborigines are to Australia)
KOROBELA: bewitching through food (to earn a beloved man/woman's
   undying affections)

LOXION: slang for location/township

MAKHULU: grandmother
MALUMES: uncles
MAMGOBOZI: gossips

MANDINGO: West African tribe popularised by Alex Haley's book 'Roots'
MAPERTUNIA, NDIYACELA UCHEL'I UMNTWANA LO: Pertunia's mother, please tell this child …
MAWEE: mother
MEISIES: (Afrikaans) girls/ladies
MNTANAMI: my child
MOS: (Afrikaans slang) isn't it/you know

NDIYACELA: I beg you/request you
NDIYADLALA: just kidding/joking
NDIYAXOLISA: I apologise
NOGAL: (Afrikaans slang) what's more
NOMAKANJANI: no matter what

OUK: (Afrikaans slang) man

PICCANIN BAAS: (derogatory slang) small black boy, 'boss'
PLAASMEISIE: (Afrikaans) farm girl
POI: Hawaiian staple

SIFUNE MUHLALE FOUR FOUR: we want you to sit four four (a common request by taxi drivers on taxi seats meant for three people)
S'RIGHT S'THANDO?: are we alright love? is that alright love?
SIS'WAM: my sister
S'THANDO SAMI: my love
STUKKEND: a lot

TATA: father
THIXO: heavens/God
TSHO: expression denoting surprise

UMAOLE: (tsotsitaal) 'maole lady', my old lady/mother
UMKONTO WE SIZWE: also known as MK, the ANC military wing. Literally translated, 'Spear of the Nation'
UYANDISOKOLISA [UNOSIZWE]: troubles/bothers [of Nosizwe]
UYAZINI: you know what?
UZAZIYENZI UCLEVAH: you think you are clever (clevah is tsotsitaal)

WENA [MANDLA] MFANA: you young man
WOOLLIES: Woolworths

UYANDISOKOLISA UNOSIZWE: Nosizwe troubles/bothers/worries me

YINI MANJE: what is it now?
YINI MANJE SQUEEZA?: what is it daughter/sister-in-law

ZOL: marijuana or a marijuana joint